Shard.

WOUNDS TO WARRIOR

Salimatou Baldé

Shard.

Wounds to Warrior

Salimatou Balde

This book is a work of fiction rooted in the author's real-life lessons and experiences.

Names, characters, places, and incidents either are products of the author's imagination or are used fictitiously.

No identification of actual events, persons (living or deceased), places, buildings, or products is intended or should be inferred.

Contact the author at: welcome@gifted-experiences.com

Dedication

To my family —
Maman, Diaraye, Assia, Siradiou —
Your presence, belief in me, and love are my anchor.
You've always challenged me to reach higher, to go beyond limits, and to believe.
This path would still be cloaked in darkness without you.
Papa, for being the first one to plant in me the love of books and the power of words.

To Olivia F., Joseph F., Jenny P. and Michael E. —
Exceptional individuals who have greatly shaped my path.
I am lucky to call you lifelong mentors.
Thank you for your steady, unwavering trust.

To My Own Hardships, including Sickle Cell Disease —
Through twisted means, you taught me resilience.
Would I have ever written without you?

And to the gifted community —
Those who carry brilliance and burdens alike.
This book is for you.
For all of you who wake up each day and turn your scars into strength.

Acknowledgments

To **Janelle** and **Winston** —
 My editors and publishers — thank you for your trust,
vision, and belief in this journey.

To **Sienna** and **Kira** —
 for your creative spark and art that helped shape this story.

To my closest friends
 Elodie, **Doryanne**, and **Alexis** —
 Your unwavering support, loyalty, and encouragement
have been a constant light over the years.

Table of Contents

Prologue

The third time it happened, Nysa could no longer ignore it.

That tingle beneath her skin—a sensation too precise, too familiar to dismiss as random—had come once, then again.

The first time, she'd brushed it off.
 The second, she'd tugged her sleeve down and whispered to herself, *"It's nothing."*

But this time—
 This third time—
 When a splash of melting ice cream landed directly on the scars along her forearm, something stirred.
 Something... responded.

She froze.

No one else seemed to notice.
 Around her, the world spun on—sunlight bouncing off windows, a breeze curling through elm branches, and an old ice cream truck humming a lullaby of summers past.

Her fingers slipped into her pocket, closing tightly around the worn, ear-shaped scrap of cotton. It grounded her, somehow.

The tune from the truck—off-key and sweet—was the same her grandmother used to hum. Soothing. Strange.

And for a moment, everything softened.

Children's laughter popped like fireworks nearby.
A squeal, a scoop hitting pavement, strawberry cream oozing toward her shoes.

A smirk—barely there—touched her lips.
Her eyes fluttered shut. She inhaled deeply: sugar, sun, and the faded scent of rain on warm concrete.
She imagined the sunlight soaking into her skin, threading into her ribs, anchoring itself somewhere beneath the surface.

Had it always felt like this?

She opened her eyes, swayed slightly. Her feet were on the sidewalk. Her body was here. But inside, something had tilted. Something old. Something watching.

Two curly-haired children bumped into her legs, startled.
One looked up at her, eyes round and glossy.
"Oh! Sorry!" the smaller one sniffled.

Nysa crouched, wiped the sticky syrup from her arm, and gently brushed the child's cheek.
"It's okay," she said softly.
The little one smiled—gummy, gap-toothed, radiant.

As Nysa stood, her sleeve slid back down, covering the scars. But the tingling didn't stop.

A tightness pulled across her chest. Her breath caught—not just from the rush of heading to Maisha's, but from something deeper.

Something was shifting.

She crossed the street quickly, her thoughts knotted in sunlight, scars, syrup—and a single question echoing louder than ever:

What stirs when the hollow cracks?

I.

*"What stirs when the hollow
cracks?"*

1.

"One turn right, fifty meters towards the billboard, and find the wooden staircase on RedBricks Avenue. Climb to the second floor." Catching her breath as she pushes the heavy wooden door, she pulls her jacket tighter around her shoulders and steps into the dimly lit apartment.

"You made it" a round yet airy voice cuts through the quiet.

Without answering, she removes her shoes and places them on the rough, U-shaped cabinet crafted from leatherwood. The scent of wood spice fades into warm vanilla as she moves down the corridor, her thoughts racing. *Something is changing. Something is different. But what is it? Is it just me? This place looks like it did before, but something is still different.*

The sound of Maisha scraping vanilla beans reaches her before she sees her—craftsmanship, only she possesses.

Leaning against the doorway of the living room, colored in shades of beige and green, she watches Maisha, who gestures towards the cozy chair beside her, a steaming teapot in hand.

"What about your jacket? Will you not take it off?" the middle-aged woman asks.

Hesitation. Instinctively, Nysa wraps her arms tightly around herself, the soft cotton feeling like a shield. Her fingers free strands from the zipper and run through her dry hair, finding reassurance in its texture. Silently, she steps towards the dark terracotta library, where a well-worn book falls into her arms—the ripped cover, a testament to the passage of time, offering no escape.

Dropping her jacket, she moves towards the chair, her bare feet feeling the grooves of the wooden floor. "Strawberry," Maisha murmurs, pouring the ideally steeped vanilla rooibos, her silver rock pendant catching the light.

"The other day, it was chocolate, on your arm, wasn't it, Nysa?"

Nysa smiles gently, her chubby body sinking into the velvety fabric of the chair, feeling as if she's floating. "Impressive, Maisha, how you always remember everything..."

"Here, to wipe your arm. You still have some cream left," Maisha says, offering a tissue.

Nysa wipes her arm, her gaze locked with Maisha's—her almond-shaped eyes reflecting a depth borne of too much seen.

Sipping her tea, Nysa tries to imprint this scene in her mind, envisioning a future just like this. "Same place, same tea," she sneezes, adding, "same smell!"

"If you only learnt to see," Maisha's voice deepens, resonant. "You could have everything you truly want. This," she gestures subtly towards the tea, "and so much more."

With a tap on the shoulder, Maisha advises, "There's water in the entrance for when you leave. Don't worry about the tea; I'll clean up."

Leaving the room, Maisha takes the warmth with her, leaving a heavy silence. As if the bright energy of the room had also vanished. A feeling all too familiar, of being around others and yet still being alone. Nysa casts one last glance at the empty chair, Maisha's words lingering, "If you only learnt to see," as if waiting for her to grasp their meaning.

She leaves a bag of candies on the table, grabs a bottle of water, and exhales deeply. *What is there to see? All is well...* She steps out into the cooler air, secretly relieved to head towards work.

2.

"11:24 AM. Perfect."

She rarely has time, but today, for once, she feels like taking it. Moving without urgency. Revived by the tea, energized by the crowded streets and noise around her, she slides her worn-out camel hobo bag on her shoulder, unzips it to grab one of her many handmade sketchbooks—excited to start her once in a blue moon, beloved activity: turning blank space into life, through her art.

As she sketches, three teenagers racing on their skates, all teeth out, inspire her first pencil strokes. Their legs shaking, betraying their nervousness to fall, she captures the fleeting beauty of their youthful recklessness. Nearby, a grey-haired man tenderly handling a watch while adjusting his retro black-rimmed glasses warms her heart and enriches her drawings. More scratches, more strokes.

While sketching, she feels the wind behind her neck, and her feet move faster to the beat of the scratches on her paper. Her shoulder, leaning and popping. Her hips, drawing large circles in the air. Imperceptibly glances around her. She sees the crowd, but the crowd does not see her, too busy to carry on. Hip to the left, right, left... and 5,6,7,8. Before her eyes, the steps of her latest choreography emerge. Her legs follow the internal beat dictated by her pulse. By the sound of the wind, turned stronger. By the honks of hurried cars. Her feet engage in a shuffle step. Choreographing. Bringing things to life through movement and music. Her thing. What she thrives in and what makes her feel most alive.

A stray paper detaches from the sketchbook at the wind's blow and starts dancing around her, as if mimicking every step she is taking. As if occupying the place of an invisible partner. She pauses for a second, fuzzies in her chest. Stares in silence at the paper bouncing until it's fallen flat on the ground. She reaches for her phone in her pocket and activates the "Do not disturb" mode, a mischievous smile on her lips, as if she could hear the voices of her friends resonating with despair, at her usual non-responsiveness. Puts on her EarPods. Spotify. Library. Liked songs. Shuffle play.

Michael Jackson's *Thriller* plays.

Her fingers tap on her pencil. She quickly closes the sketchbook, catching the flying, free-spirited pieces of paper in their attempt to escape, and puts them back in her bag. She takes her jacket out and throws it on her shoulders, satisfied with the extra layer of movement available for her choreography. Her body feels lighter and lighter. The world around her, vibrant. Faces of strangers, smiling right back at her.

Conscious of the gaze of pedestrians on her, her fingers fidget on the EarPods, which she takes off abruptly. Silence.

A second to focus. Noise again.

The crowd's attention already drawn elsewhere, she rubs her palms on her pants, the moisture on her hands slowly fading into the bleached jeans fabric. She reaches for her phone and hovers over "Do not disturb". Thoughts are back, flooding her mind. Her heartbeat slows down, as her steps do, too. She throws a look at her phone in her hand, and her heart skips a beat.

Something on her screen catches her attention. A shape. Or, a shadow. Her lungs hold her breath before she does. A whisper in her ear. Instinctively, she reaches for her bag and the water inside. Quick! Fluidity feels like safety. As always, she drinks three sips, exhales, and inhales. Feels the drops flowing down her throat. Through her veins.

Ok. Thoughts gathered.

Hesitant to turn around, she lifts her phone straight in front of her and looks into the mirror conveniently offered by her glass screen protection. Movement. And then, nothing. And, a shadow.

Hastening, she crosses the street to the busiest side, the knot in her stomach untying, her heartbeat slowing down at the feeling of safety provided by the crowd. *What's wrong with you now... girl, you need some serious sleep!* she thinks, laughing inside. Increasing her pace to the Liapsar Boulevard, turning right on Serves Street, she finally sees it. 270 meters ahead: The Center. A modern four-floored, glass and wooden building with a climbing plant façade, and a flat ceiling. Her second home, and one of her most cherished places in the world. The Center of her universe, where magic happens. Where she teaches young, ambitious dancers to conquer their bodies through music and the world through the perfection of dances.

As she reaches the laminated glass front door of The Center, she sighs at her reflection. She enters the building, and soothes into comfort, as the warm and lively feeling so typical of entering the place, awakens in her stomach.

Memories of her four years ago, stepping into the airy lobby for the first time, stream through her mind. In the middle of a crisis that caused her to lose her job and romantic relationship altogether, The Center, with its cosy furniture and natural light, comforted her body and soul with warmth. *A place that makes everyone feel at home. No discrimination.*

Behind a majestic white marble spiral staircase, two elevators facing each other delimit the area dedicated to photos of famous alumni, called by many the Wall of Fame. In the middle of it all, a sepia picture of a young athlete swirling under a thunderstorm starts coming off the wall.

She presses it back and watches it fall off as she enters the lift for the fourth floor.

One last sip of water before it gets hectic. She grabs the bottle from her bag and swallows the last drops, gets out of the elevator, and throws it in the yellow bin. A wrinkled piece of paper falls out, misplaced. "When are these students going to learn? Paper goes into the blue bin..." She picks up the paper and takes a look at the black and white ad picturing the inside of an old movie theater. In the center, a scene is playing on a screen, subtitled:

How long can one run before running out?

She rolls the paper into a ball, throws it in the bin with a nod, and retraces her steps to Studio 4-202, from where tremendous hubbub emanates.

3.

When Nysa steps into her studio, she freezes. The room is filled with unbearable shouting and loud laughter.

"Guys!" she shouts, her voice lost in the cacophony.

Elbowing her way through the crowd of young dancers, she finally sees the cause of the chaos on her sacred blackboard—a name that sends a shiver down her spine: THORNE.

The prodigy dancer, a legend whose disappearance left a void in the dance world. To others, his name might evoke admiration, desire, or envy. To Nysa, it spelled pure waste—a squandered gift.

The room buzzes with wild speculations:

"I cannot believe he is back..." "...hurt his partner really bad..." "...controls storms..." "...shadow fades under the sun..." "...lost the love of his life..."

"Everyone! Silence! Now!!" Nysa commands, her finger pointing accusingly at the blackboard.

The room falls into a hushed whisper.

"Apologies. I surely can explain."

From the crowd emerges a tall, frail silhouette. Thorne. The same man from the sepia photo that had fallen earlier, yet starkly different in reality—pale, fragile.

He approaches, offering a handshake. "I arrived last night. I was eager to meet you, Nysa. Is that correct? Pleasure to meet you."

His gaze drops to his hand, adding, "I assure you, it will not break from a firm handshake."

Perturbed, Nysa hesitates but finally grasps his hand. The touch sends an unexpected jolt through her—his grip firm yet strangely comforting, enveloping her in an unsettling familiarity. *No... Something is off...*

The room's light flickers, mirroring her disorientation.

"Nysa. Pleasure," she manages to reply, her mind racing.

"I will see you later, Nysa," Thorne says, his departure as smooth as his entrance.

Nysa tries to refocus. "Class of 3rd year, fusion routine, from the top!" She attempts to regain control, but her thoughts are elsewhere.

This arrogance... I know I have met him before...

Unable to focus, she welcomes the ringing bell with gratitude and halts the music. "This is all for today."

Class empty, she rushes out, bypassing the elevator for the stairs, driven by a need to escape. As she exits the building, her mind reels.

"WHO the hell is this man? Who does he think he is, stepping into my studio like that?"

She finds a bench outside, sitting to calm her racing heart. "What is happening to me? Thorne, living legend or not, you stay the hell away from me..."

4.

When Nysa stirs from the bench, the sun had long set. Hours might have passed—two, three, or more. Chilled to the bone, her fingers stiffen against the damp wood of the bench.

Groggily standing, she feels an unsettling burn in her forearms, her body's temperature strangely skewed. The glaring night lights of The Center blind her momentarily as she heads back, ignoring the dizziness and the inner voice cautioning her to rest. *No pain, no gain, Nysa.*

Inside The Center, she ascends to the fourth floor, her burning arm throbbing with each step. In studio 4-202, she blasts the music to its highest volume, trying to drown out her inner turmoil with external noise—anger, pain, loneliness echoing in the loudness.

Barefoot on the cold floor, she dances, her body momentarily forgetting the pain. Twirls and hops flow perfectly as always, until—"Ouch!"—her ankle twists, sending her crashing to the floor. Pain shoots up her leg as she clutches her ankle, her elbow reddening from another fall. *I've fallen before, but it's never felt like this.*

Struggling to stand, she whispers encouragement to herself, "Good job, legs," before another wave of pain takes her down. The phone rings unnoticed, its soft melody lost under the blaring music and the rush of blood in her ears. Only the flashing light of a missed call catches her eye, the phone lying frustratingly out of reach.

Crawling with great effort, she curses through clenched teeth, each movement a fiery agony. The tingling in her forearm intensifies, merging with the heat radiating from her forehead. She tries standing again, her breaths short and ragged, the world tilting dangerously.

Then, the fall feels soft, unexpectedly safe. Thorne's arms are around her, a gentle but firm presence. A tear escapes her eye as she meets his gaze—*was that thunder in his eyes?*

"Let me," she murmurs weakly. "Don't touch me!" she protests as he carefully lays her down and covers her with her jacket. He turns off the music and dims the lights, his silhouette framed by the moonlight as he watches her momentarily before leaving.

Curled up on the floor, Nysa counts her breaths to steady herself, her finger tracing circles on her forearm. The room quiets to a whisper, her energy is spent.

Thorne pauses at the door, his hands warm from the contact. "One only has one body, Nysa. How can you not get what yours is telling you..." He mutters before disappearing into the night.

Alone, Nysa opens her eyes, refusing the weak reflection staring back at her from the mirror. *So weak... No. This cannot be me.* The tingle grows, a palpable presence whispering to her bones. She stands despite the pain. She is now summoned back to the space she hates, but is the only one she can turn to in her fear, loneliness, and dread.

Stuck between two betrayals: The one of going back because she promised herself she would never. And the other, of letting her body down if she doesn't go, because she knows she has to, to get better.

5.

Moments later
In an old Greek battle arena, known as The Ancient Place

My feet know the way before my mind does.
Despite my vows never to return, I find myself drawn back to that haunting place. The place I despise more than any other. Where my weakness is revealed.

I feel my tears rolling down my cheeks, and the burning pain in my limbs as I stumble against the rough stone wall. The air is thick with familiarity—the scent, the hues, the textures all etched deep within my subconscious like indelible ink.

Without a thought, I shed my jacket and press my forearms against the cold, damp clay, fiercely wiping the tears away with the back of my hand.

"What will it be today? What will it demand in return?" I ask silently, before collapsing to the ground.

Time slows as I lie on the floor, and haze envelops my sedated mind. I feel the spasms in my body. Pain. Anger. At life. At everyone. At God.

For such hardships. For making life so difficult.

Time passes, I cannot tell how much. I somehow manage to prop myself on my elbows, twist to lie back, and face the sky.

My body moves instinctively, as if choreographed by unseen forces. Repeating the familiar, dreadful ritual. Same as every time. For as many years as I can remember.

My temperature plummets, my breath becomes shards of ice. I can't breathe. Each inhalation stabs at my lungs. I lose control over my body, over my voice. They break.

I slide my hand in my pocket, for the old cotton piece —it is gone.

I clench my fists and cease all movement. *Breathe, lungs...* I hear myself thinking. But they cannot.

My bones feel like... they are being chiseled at by invisible hammers. My veins collapse, and oxygen ceases to flow.
I cry silent tears, and my mind starts to drift.
To detach and float away.

I feel cold. I am freezing. And burning. Like fire. Something stirs within me, terrifying. But familiar.

—And then, all noises cease. There is only silence.

My head lifts, my throat gasps for air as if I were surfacing from deep water. I feel my heart stiffen, my blood thicken and clot. My feet turn to ice, my bones crack and crumble.

And in my mind, all I can think of is God. *Will you help me again?*

A lethal sliver of glass, sharp as a sickle, scrapes along my veins. My mind goes blank. The pain, excruciating. Searing.

And I do, like always, when the challenge feels too high. I allow my spirit to rise. Hover above her body, desperate for release from the torment.

And time...

freezes.

My eyes open again. Slowly. I feel some air, finally flowing in. Life seeps back into my cells, oxygen rushes through my veins. The pain is now tempered.
How much does one need to endure, just to be deemed strong?...

My forearms burn, and I can hear my screams piercing the night. Yet, I feel unheard.

My eyes are on fire, but inside... emptiness. I surrender.
My breath steadies, my eyes shut, and I fall into numbness.

When I wake up, I can't tell how much time has passed. A sharp sensation—smoke, not just wind, assaults me. I blink, confused by the haze. "Where am I?"
I sit up. The timid crepuscular rays caressing my skin finish waking me up. "Here. I had to come back." I recall all of it.

I stand, turn slowly, look around, survey my surroundings—an ancient arena, reminding me of old Greek battlegrounds, its age etched in every stone and smoke plume spiraling from the stained walls.
The ground is littered with timeless rocks; where I leaned earlier, tiny dots of my blood seem forever imprinted on the wall. The vision of it makes me shiver.

I shake my head, and the uncomfortable feeling that arises in my chest. "Creepy".
This place always creeped me out.

Like always, I start a body scan.

Have you ever tried it? What works for you, dear reader, when you feel unsettled? Unbalanced, or losing control?

For me, this is a tried and true method that helps to reconnect my mind and body. Regain control.

I look down at my feet. Start from the bottom.

Slowly move the tip of my toes. "Ok, working well".
Press the back of my feet against the ground, reconnect to the earth. "Ok, working too".
Then, my knees and hips. Their strength holds me up. "Thank God, working."
My lower back. Tension release, "Ok, supple."
My upper chest... My diaphragm moves up... and down... "Ok."

I exhale loudly, relieved. I am well.

Satisfied with the state of my body and the health of my organs, I grab my phone lying in the mud.

Two missed calls from Maisha. I turn back to the wall one last time, ready to leave. Such a strange place.
To an outsider, it appears as nothing more than an old

stone park. But to me, it has always been something else. A place where ancient echoes meet the present. Repulsive. But strangely healing.

The sunlight dims, clouds gather above my head, and the sudden gust stirs more smoke from the wall. Before my eyes, the blood dots on the wall connect into thin dark lines, forming a terrifying question:

Until when can one pretend and betray?

"Not now." The words almost escape my lips.

My phone slips from my trembling hands, as a knot forms in my stomach.

I shake my head. Thought I had escaped this question.

The marks on her skin redden. Burning.

I pick up the phone, shake off the sinister energy.

Brush off the mud, tap my screen, and hover over Maisha's name. The voice inside my head immediately jumps in: *No. I don't want anyone to see me like this.*

I turn off my phone and walk towards the exit. *How much longer can I stand this?*

UNTIL WHEN CAN ONE PRETEND AND BETRAY

II.

"What is seen when the veil is gone?"

6.

Hours later
11:03 PM – Nysa's Home, 610 Greenhole Square

Home, Nysa lies in her bed, physically and emotionally exhausted. *Last night was not easy.* The blanket pulled up to her chin, her room is dimly lit to match the heaviness settling in her heart, her body no longer something she feels owns. Eyes reddened from tears and exhaustion, her arm reaches out under a pile of unused pillows, which she uses as a poor excuse for human contact. She finds the piece of warm, worn cotton she keeps hidden away. Her fingers close around it, drawing it close to her chest.

She stares at it in the quiet of her room, rolling the frayed, downy ear through her fingers. It is soft but torn, its grey fabric holding the musty scent of years gone by—a tangible reminder of her past struggles and the comfort they once provided.

She heaves a deep sigh, her grip tightening. "I know... what does not break you makes you rise. I know," she whispers to the silent room, finding a melancholy strength in the words.

Her heart, heavy yet gradually calming, seems to sync with the slow, rhythmic sound of the night outside her window. She turns off the bedside lamp, the last flicker of light fading into darkness. In her mind, a silent vow to herself to rise again, despite the shadows that loom both within and beyond her walls.

The next day
10:46 AM – Meeting point: a fashion boutique

Nysa inhales deeply, allowing a moment of silence to envelop her body and mind as she touches the fabric of the high-waist, long mesh skirt with an open front. The texture is soothing, soft, and delicate under her fingers, its lilac scent lingering in the air, subtly calming her racing heart. Despite the comfort the clothes provide, she feels discord within herself.

Until when can one pretend and betray... the words continue to echo in her mind, their weight oppressive on her soul.

"...Ma'am? A different size?" the shop assistant's voice cut through her reverie.

"Yes, one size smaller, please. I'll take it" she responds quickly, her voice brighter than she feels.

She grabs her phone, scans her fingerprint, and snaps a selfie with the 'Dramatic Warm' filter.

```
Giving off 'cool professor with some swag'
vibes  😛," she types, trying to inject some lightness
into her day.
```

Maisha's reply, prompt but neutral:

```
"Almost there, was delayed. Wait for me."
```

Hmmm... She did not comment. Maybe it doesn't suit me... Nysa muses, feeling momentarily disconnected from everything around her. She shakes off the feeling, pulling a silky scarf from a hanger and draping it around her neck. She removes her scrunchie, letting her hair fall freely, and takes another photo.

```
"What about now? Much better than the
'old-bones, moody lady' look!"
```
she considers before erasing and retyping her message with an added: "😂."

No immediate response comes. Sighing, she admires the refreshing shades of orange of the scarf against her neck in the mirror, but soon removes it and returns everything to its hangers. As she exits the fitting room, she hands her selections to the assistant with a gentle shake of her head.

"Not even the scarf?" Maisha asks from behind her, catching up. "That is a good color on you."

She hesitates, then concedes, "Or... Ok. I'll take it."

As she reaches for her credit card, a cold draft sweeps through the boutique as the door opens, allowing a new customer in and pulling her joy out with it.

"Well, that was fun, wasn't it. But we should go now" she remarks to Maisha, her tone light but strained. She adjusts her scrunchie and slouches her shoulders, exhaling deeply as she glances at her reflection.

Back to normal.
Yet not quite.

Feeling Maisha's warm hand on her arm as they leave the boutique together, Nysa allows herself a small comfort in the familiarity, their minds heavy with unspoken thoughts.

As they dash through the crowded streets, Maisha's grip tightens around Nysa's hand. Abruptly, Nysa halts, her gaze fixed on an electronic billboard flickering in the distance.

7.

Amidst the pulsing lights, a shadow catches her eye, drawing her entire focus.

She tilts her head back, her heart pounding as the screen clears to reveal The Center —*her* Center—, now swarming with journalists. Amid the chaos, there he is—Thorne, microphones thrust toward him by a sea of eager reporters.

Her breath caught in her throat, a visceral reaction tightening her stomach as if punched. The air around her seems to thicken, time slowing to a crawl.

Maisha, sensing the shift, turns to look at her, concern etching her features. "What is your gut telling you?" she asks, her voice a low murmur over the noise of the city.

Nysa can't form words, the sight of Thorne triggering a storm of emotions and memories. Without a word, she grasps Maisha's arm with a firm urgency and pulls her forward. They resume running, weaving through the bustling crowd, the image of Thorne burned into Nysa's mind, igniting fears and questions she would rather dismiss.

As they move, the sounds of the city meld into a distant blur, Nysa's thoughts racing faster than their sprinting feet. The unexpected sight of Thorne in such a public and powerful context, a jolt that shakes her to her core, leaving her to wrestle with a whirlwind of implications as they disappear into the throng.

She bursts through the glass doors of The Center, immediately feeling the absence of its usually warm and lively ambiance. The air is charged, almost electric, as if the normal rhythm of the place has been disrupted by a storm.

Thorne stands on stage, illuminated not just by the stage lights but also by the relentless flashes from dozens of cameras. He is the epitome of authority and charisma, radiating an almost sun-like brilliance that commands the room.

"Who is... How is that possible?" Nysa murmurs, her voice a mix of awe and disbelief.

Turning to Maisha, she continues, "He looks... different. Bigger again. Like in his old pictures, not at all like the frail man I saw earlier."

Her stomach knots, and her legs feel like they were encased in ice, the room's air seemingly sucked away by Thorne's presence.

Thorne's voice booms across the room, authoritative yet smooth, "...and finally, to the question of why I returned, can one ever truly escape who they are? Let's just say, it was high time I came home."

His gaze sweeps across the audience, locking onto Nysa's. He smiles slightly, an acknowledgment full of unsaid words.

Journalists clamor for his attention, their questions blending into a cacophony of curiosity and accusation: "Mister Thorne, were you expelled after founding The Center?" "Have you been secretly dancing across Europe and Asia?" "Tell us about the rumors of your stay at Johns Hopkins' Psychiatric Care Unit." "Is that really you with your supposed ex-wife on Instagram?"

The hubbub grows louder, but Nysa can barely hear it over the pounding of her heart. She is transfixed, pulled in by Thorne's commanding presence.

Finally breaking the gaze, she turns to Maisha, shaking her head as if to clear it. "Errrh, how can he be so... What? What are you looking at?"

Maisha glances at the stage, a subtle light flashing in her eyes. "Hmm. Nothing," she replies. With a hint of irony, she adds, "Isn't this the center that welcomes everyone?"

Nysa's eyes reddened, her emotions brimming to the surface. "No! This is MY home here, and..."

Maisha cuts her off, her hand raised in a calming gesture, "Needless to speak, young lady. Come. You're staying at my place tonight."

8.

That night
Much, much later – Maisha's home, 7 RedBricks Avenue

Silent as a shadow, Maisha tiptoes to the guest room's door, her ear pressed gently against the wood. Whispering, her voice tinged with concern, she murmurs, "Nysa, dear, what is it that you fear?" No response comes, only the unsettling sounds of distress from the young woman tossing in her sleep inside. Sighing deeply, Maisha leans her back against the door, feeling a twist in her stomach as she absorbs the palpable anguish seeping through.

Inside the room, Nysa finds herself lost in a haunting dreamscape:

"Where am I?"
 The thought forms in my mind, foggy and distant, as if I'm caught between waking and dreaming—trapped in something deep.

I look around, but nothing feels familiar. I'm in a corridor—long, dark, and unbearably narrow. The air presses in on me, thick with humidity and dust, almost unbreathable. My lungs protest, but I can't stop inhaling. Something drips steadily from the ceiling—water, I think—each drop echoing like a countdown. Flickering lanterns hang on the damp stone walls, casting trembling shadows. The stench of sewage is overwhelming, thick enough to taste.

I try to hold my breath, but my throat disobeys. My stomach convulses, and before I can stop it, I double over and vomit. My knees threaten to give out, but I steady myself. Wiping my mouth with the back of my hand, I straighten up, shaky. The walls feel too close. I stretch my arms out—they nearly touch both sides. Rough stone brushes against my sleeves, and the claustrophobia hits me hard, tightening like a rope around my chest.

I squint into the dark. My vision adjusts slowly. One cautious step forward. Another. My movements are deliberate, but my feet—there's a strange familiarity in the way they move. It's like they've been here before, like they know something I don't. My palms glide over the walls, searching—feeling the cracks, but no escape.

A glint of light catches my eye. One of the lanterns flickers more brightly ahead, revealing something—a shape. Rectangular. Metallic? Glass? Ten meters away, maybe. I step closer, curiosity battling the dread crawling up my spine.

It's a mirror. Tall. Ancient. Sharp-edged and heavy-looking, leaning against the wall like it's been waiting for me. Its surface is smeared with dust and mold, dull and lifeless. No reflection—just darkness.

I inch forward. Still nothing—no image of me. It's like I'm not here. Or like the mirror doesn't recognize me.

Then—
Clink.

Something hits the floor, far off. I freeze, straining to hear. I look up. There, beside the mirror. A figure. Small. Human. A child.

Standing there. Staring at me.

I blink. Gone.

I blink again. And now—they're *inside* the mirror.

I don't know how I know it's the same child, but I do. Their gaze, locked with mine, is chilling. They look fragile. Sickly. Skin pale, ribs visible beneath a ripped, filthy shirt. A tremor crawls up my arms. I wrap them around myself, but my jacket is no help against the sudden cold sweeping through the corridor. The air turns glacial. I can feel the hair rise beneath my sleeves.

Still, I can't look away.

My heart slams against my ribs as if trying to escape. The silence is unbearable—so full of weight, like it's trying to crush me with all the things unsaid. I whisper, barely able to find my voice:

"Who are you?"

The child doesn't move. Doesn't blink. Just watches.

I take a step forward. My arms tingle, nerves alive with electricity. Fear and something else—something ancient and sharp. The lanterns go out.

And the mirror—
  Crack.

A split runs through the glass.

Another.
  More.

Then—*shatter.*

It explodes outward. Shards slice through the air, slashing into my skin—my legs, my arms. I gasp from the pain, shielding my face. The cuts burn hot. Around me, glass rains down, glinting like stars falling too fast.

But the child... remains.

Still. Unflinching. Watching.

A glint flashes in their eye. A flicker—something not quite human. And then, as suddenly as they came, they vanish.

The corridor falls into silence again.

I'm alone. Cut. Bleeding. Cold.

I glance down. The mirror is gone, but its fragments remain, scattered around me. Some still reflect pieces of me—my arms, my face—warped and trembling. I press my hands to my chest. My heart is racing so fast it hurts.

I look into the shards and whisper, to no one and to everything:

"I will be back."

Outside the room, Maisha, still leaning against the door, shudders as another moan of torment escapes from within, her worry for Nysa deepening with each passing moment. *Something is changing within her. I should have seen this coming. Maybe, I could have saved her from this pain...*

Waking, Nysa gasps for air, her breath ragged as she clutches at the sheets. She rubs her feet together vigorously, trying to generate warmth, and wraps her arms tightly around her knees, her body shivering uncontrollably. The comforting warmth of her blanket feels surreal, almost as if it belonged to another reality.

Noticing the faint shadow cast by the light under her door, she whispers a prayer of gratitude, her voice trembling. "Maisha..." The presence of her friend nearby, a small comfort against the lingering terror of her dream.

Her heart thuds painfully in her chest as she holds her breath for a moment and releases it slowly. The imagined pain where the dream's glass shards cut her feels almost real. "I do not need to look, I know there is nothing. Stop freaking out, Nysa, it was just a bad dream" she mutters to herself.

The room still feels unnaturally cold, and she pulls the blanket tighter around her, covering her neck. Rubbing her eyes wearily, she yawns and shifts into a sitting position. As her pulse begins to slow, her mind can't help but wander back to the vivid images of the dream. *Those eyes, that child in the mirror... The way they looked at me... And the marks on my arms, they were... glowing? Moving?*

Compelled by a nagging doubt, she glances down at her arms, half-expecting to see something. But there is nothing—just her skin, unmarked and ordinary. Relieved yet unsettled, she settles back against her pillows.

And then, a startling discovery: as her eyes adjust to the dim light, she notices tiny red dots on her skin, connected by thin, dark red lines. She stares, her mind racing as the markings form a question:

What... shapes, yet... remains... unseen?

9.

Eyes fixed on her arms where the cryptic lines had vanished, Nysa whispers, a hint of desperation in her voice, "Am I turning crazy?" The question hangs in the air, heavy.

Lying on her back, she tries to calm the turmoil within by focusing on her breathing. Placing a palm over her heart, she inhales deeply, holds her breath for a moment, and exhales slowly. Again, she inhales, holds...

—startled by the sudden buzz of her phone. Her heart leaps, and the fragile serenity shatters. Turning towards the nightstand, her movements quick, she reaches out and grabs the phone.

The screen lights up to reveal a photo taken in room 4-202, accompanied by a terse message:

```
We need to meet. ASAP.
~ T
```

Nysa stares at the message, her mind racing. *What does Thorne know? Why does he keep intruding into my studio?*

But as she ponders, the message disappears from the screen.
3 seconds. 2. 1.
Gone.
As if it had never been there.

10.

In the dim morning light, Nysa lies still, the message from Thorne replaying incessantly in her mind. Eyes wide open, she traces circles around the dark bags under her eyes with her fingertips, staring blankly at the ceiling where timid rays of sun begin to brighten the beige paint. The air feels unexpectedly light around her, in stark contrast to the heaviness of her own body.

Holding her phone, the messaging app still open, she reaches for the glass of water on her nightstand and takes a slow sip, trying to wash down the sensation that sits in her stomach.

With a sigh, she pushes herself up on her elbows and swings her legs out. Standing before the mirror, she examines her reflection closely. Her forearm looks just as it had always been—intact, with no trace of the tiny dots of blood or the cryptic message that had seemed so real in her dream.

Studying her own eyes in the mirror, she cringes at the emptiness reflecting back at her. Placing a hand on her stomach, she lets out a deep sigh and attempts a smile. Grabbing her hoodie, she drags herself out of the room and heads towards Maisha's door.

"Maisha! Thanks for letting me stay here. Could I talk to you?" she calls out, knocking lightly.

There is no response.

Pausing with her fist still raised to the door, she exhales deeply and leans in to listen. Silence. Pulling back, she tiptoes to the entrance, feeling a weight pressing on her chest.

With a determined look, she makes her way out of the apartment.

Her first stop: the Director's office at The Center to address the Thorne situation.

"I am surprised, Nysa: our students are delighted, and so is the entire teaching body. You are a wonderful teacher, and The Center holds you in a special place, just as I know you cherish it too. But you must remember, Thorne founded this place. You will need to learn to work together if you want to continue teaching this semester," Director Wolehead's words echoed in her mind. "I've asked him to join your class again this afternoon for a short demo in the amphitheater. Can I trust that you two will get along?"

"But, Mister Wolehead... Forget it. Yes, we will" she replies, her voice a mixture of resignation and frustration.

Heading to the amphitheater on the second floor, Nysa plugs in her EarPods, letting the pulsating beat of Rihanna's *What's My Name* drown out the lingering thoughts of rebellion sparked by her conversation with the Director.

Arriving early and alone, she activates the powerful HiFi stereo speakers positioned at both ends of the amphitheater, connects to her playlist, and immerses herself in the music. With a deep exhale, she closes the glass doors behind her and surrenders to the rhythm, letting the dance take over the tumult in her mind.

As soon as her body begins to move, the air around her seems to lighten. The persistent weight in her chest that had shadowed her since morning dissipates like snow under a warm sun.

Her movements are fluid and fast, embodying grace and precision as she spins, twirls, and leaps across the floor. Grabbing a chair, she incorporates it into her dance, weaving around and beneath it with the fluidity of water, her movements instinctive and sharp.

Letting her arms fly upward, she releases her hair from a scrunchie. While her face remains serious, a sense of freedom courses through her. The music envelops her soul, shutting out the world as she executes splits, bends, and double spins, her body carried as if on invisible wings. She closes her eyes and smiles, her spirit alight with the pure joy of movement.

In a moment of unbridled energy, as she swings her arm through the air, the chair unexpectedly lifts from the ground, hovering five to six centimeters before gently settling back down. She doesn't pause to consider it; her body fills with energy, her every muscle burning with the intensity of her performance.

The room around her feels alive, charged with an electric current that seems to resonate with her every move. Nysa has transformed the amphitheater into her sanctuary, a place where she can escape the complexities of her life and truly breathe through her art.

Lighter and lighter, she continues to move. Free, all alone, the world at her feet. As she dances, another chair rises into the air.

—Then two, then three... then four.

Surrounded by flying chairs, tables, and markers, she moves as if in her own universe, her eyes close, her mind blissfully shuts off from reality. Her heart races with exhilaration as she sits on the floor and rolls from side to side.

Crack. Crack.

The sound of small cracks echoe faintly, drawing her attention toward the mirror.

A cool breeze brushes her skin, sending goosebumps along her arms. She opens her eyes and, for a moment, sees the chairs suspended in the air around her. "What..." she whispers, her voice a mix of awe and confusion. She pauses, her eyes narrowing as she tries to make sense of the scene.

She rubs her eyes vigorously, shakes her head in disbelief. When she looks again, the chairs have returned to the floor, as if they had never left.

Turning around, she sees Thorne standing behind the glass door, his gaze alternating between her and the cracked mirror. The intensity in his eyes is unmistakable. He has seen everything. *What is wrong with him? I don't understand. Why is he everywhere?*

Quickly, Nysa turns off the music and grabs her jacket from the floor, feeling the familiar weight of the world settle back onto her shoulders.

She exhales a heavy sigh, her moment of supernatural freedom fading as she faces the reality of Thorne's presence. "Hey! You!" she calls out assertively, stepping toward him.

11.

"Hey! You! Stop walking!" Nysa calls out, her voice echoing down the corridor. Thorne doesn't turn; instead, he quickens his pace and enters the men's bathroom. The door crashes against the wall and slams shut behind him.

Nysa storms in after him. "What do you think you are doing, spying on me? Sending me those messages and... Hey! I'm talking to you!"

Thorne stands silent, his back to her for a moment before slowly turning to face her. His expression is unreadable, calm.

"You are going to explain yourself right now!" she yells, reaching out to grab his arm.

Ouchhh! The touch sends a jolt of pain through her hand. "Your skin is..." she gasps, the heat from his arm scorching her skin.

Mouth agape, she freezes, her eyes widening as she recognizes something terrifyingly familiar on his forearm. Clutching his arm tighter, she turns it over and sees them—tiny, burning dots, just like the ones from her dream.

A chill runs down her spine, her shoulders twitching involuntarily. His skin continues to burn into hers, but she can't pull away, transfixed by the marks that mirror her own nocturnal visions.

She lifts her gaze to meet his. Thorne stares back, unblinking, his expression softening as he slowly kneels on the floor, a heavy sigh breaking the tense silence. *No, I never wanted her to see me like this. What will she think now?* His lips remain sealed, his jaw tenses.

Acid reflux churns in her stomach, the sensation almost overwhelming. Yet, the heat from his skin is inescapable, and amidst the pain, something shifts. Connected by thin, dark red lines, a cryptic message appeared on his arm:

What is one not reading?

Just then, a knock sounds at the door, followed by the distant rumble of thunder. A voice calls from outside, "Can I come in?"

As rigid as a statue, Nysa releases Thorne's arm, casting one last deep look into his eyes. Tears well up in her own as she limps out of the bathroom, leaving behind the unanswered questions and the burning mystery that links them.

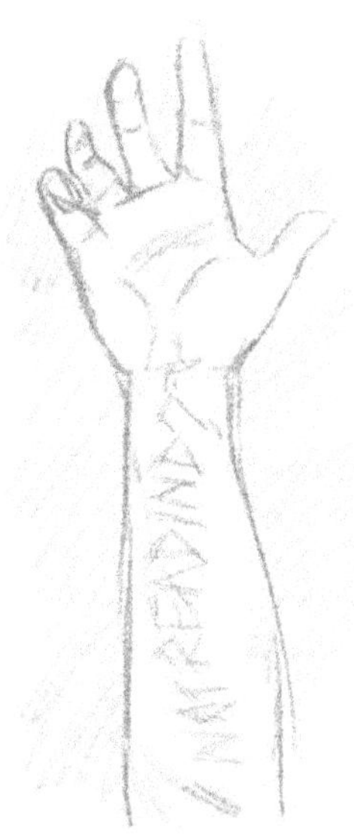

III.

"What was never meant to be carried?"

12.

The next morning
6:52 AM – The Center

Groggy from a nearly sleepless night, Nysa steps into The Center at dawn, her senses immediately tense up. Thorne is here—upstairs. She can almost smell his presence, a strange, inexplicable scent lingering in the air, resonating deep within her cells.

The usual warmth and vibrancy of The Center are conspicuously absent. The hallways, typically bright and lively, feel subdued, as if the building itself is holding its breath.

Walking past the spiral staircase, Nysa heads straight to the Wall of Fame. Her eyes are drawn to one photograph in particular, slightly peeled off at the corners: a young, athletic figure dancing boldly under a thunderstorm. Bold. Dangerous. Magnetic.

She hesitantly touches the photograph, her fingers brushing against the rugged, crackling paper. "Cracky and old," she murmurs, a trace of wonder in her voice.

Her gaze sweeps over the entire wall. *Older than all the other pictures.* She tries to press the peeling photo back

into place, holding it against the adhesive for a count—
3 seconds, 2, 1. But as soon as she lets go, the corner curls
away from the wall once more.

With a sigh of resignation, Nysa turns to leave but pauses
as something catches her eye—a glimpse of something
handwritten or drawn, beneath the peeling corner of the
photo. Leaning closer, she deciphers six numbers scrawled
there: 11.04.25.

"Eleventh of April, 2025?" she questions aloud, her brow
furrowing. "But this picture is at least twenty years old!"

Confused yet intrigued, she flattens the photo against the
wall one last time, exhaling slowly as her mind races with
the implications of the date. Shaking off the perplexity, she
ascends the stairs to the first floor.

"Hey, have you seen Marq?" she inquires of a group of
first-year students she passes.

"In studio 1-307, Professor," they reply.

Quickening her pace, Nysa reaches the studio and finds
the middle-aged custodian, Marq, sweeping the floor with
his EarPods in, blissfully singing aloud.

Nysa enters The Center at dawn, her mind clouded from
a restless night. As she approaches the familiar face tidying
up the lobby, she can't help but think. *This man... one of a*

kind. Been here taking classes for 12 years, so talented, and still refuses to leave.

Marq notices her and pulls out his EarPods with a bright smile, "Oh, Professor, hi. Didn't see you there. Can I help you with something?"

"Marq, can I access The Core?" Nysa asks, hoping to delve deeper into the mysteries that had kept her awake.

"You're in luck, Professor," Marq grins, revealing a mouth full of teeth. "The archive reopened today. I can take you there if you want—it's quite a mess, though."

"Thank you, Marq. I would appreciate that" a sense of urgency in her tone.

They walk through the silent, dimly lit corridors of The Center's basement, arriving at the door of The Core. The room is even darker and more imposing than the rest of the building.

"Here, take this flashlight. The lights are still a bit temperamental," Marq hands her a heavy flashlight. "Call me if you need anything," he adds before heading back to the elevator.

As Marq retreats, he casts one last glance towards The Core and mutters under his breath, "Something tells me this is not just a regular library to you, Professor." With a knowing smirk, he rotates his hand in the air, summoning a glittery string that floats towards the room, hinting at the deeper secrets held within. "You shall not leave without the truth," he adds in a whisper.

Flashlight in hand, Nysa begins her search through the towering shelves, whispering the annotated numbers, "11.04.25, April 2011 maybe? April 2011..." Yet, nothing matches her query.

As she turns to leave, overwhelmed by the room's oppressive darkness, a momentary thought of escape crosses her mind. Her resolve strengthens, she presses on, "Let's keep going," she mutters, stepping carefully as the floor beneath her creaks ominously.

"What about here, alumni logs?" Nysa muses, reaching a section filled with old records. She quickly finds a file labeled 'Thorne' and begins flipping through it—photographs, diplomas, evaluations, and more images of him.

One particular photo catches her attention: a familiar ancient arena, with vapors of smoke weaving through the air and a frail, emaciated child standing solemnly, a mysterious yellow ray of light shining in their eye.

As Nysa examines the photo closer, the room seems to respond; a breeze fluttered by, causing the flashlight to dim and flicker. Her eyes lock with the child's, and as the yellow light seems to pull her in, her temples throb with a sudden rush of blood.

Another flicker, and a crack—the flashlight shatters on the floor.

Instinctively, Nysa snatches the photograph from the folder, tucks it into her pocket, and dashes out of The Core, oblivious to the shadow watching her from afar, driven by a newfound urgency to confront Thorne directly.

Upon reaching room 4-202, she finds him captivating a roomful of students with his vivid recount of the birth of HipHop, his narrative spanning decades and continents, his presence as enigmatic as the photo she now carries.

13.

"Ok, I need fresh air," Nysa mutters to herself, feeling a tightness in her stomach that urges her to seek solace in the ladies' bathroom.

At this early hour, the bathroom is deserted, its vast space known for offering light and warmth to those in need of comfort. The soothing hues of luminous sandstone and ivory tiles help calm her mind and pulse, even as the hot sunrays soften her reflection in the mirror, as if stripping away more than just her rage and cluelessness— to peel layers off her very self.
Looking skinnier, yet feeling heavier.

Standing still with her face wet, her palms resting on the smooth edge of the washbasin, she stares intently at her reflection—eyes, cheeks, collarbone. With a deep exhale, she brushes her collarbone with a finger and shivers, slides the cold metallic zipper of her jacket to the top.

She takes out the picture of the child with yellow eyes from her pocket. Images and sounds from her recent experiences collide in her mind—the oppressive darkness of a room, tiny lines of blood on a wall, chairs floating, tingling marks on forearms, unheard cries in the night. "What is going on here... Is any of this real?"

Closing her eyes, her mind wanders back to those moments. Weight. Darkness. A whisper: "The price to pay."

Minutes pass in silent stillness.

When the tumult inside her finally quiets, she opens her eyes and looks around for any place to sit—a chair, a stool, anything to help carry the weight of her seemingly ton-heavy body.

She turns off the faucet, but the water continues to flow. Confused, she twists the knob again, harder this time—still no movement. Eyes narrow in bewilderment, she tests the tap on the adjacent sink. Immediately, a strong stream of water gushes forth.

Taking a few steps back, she watches the anomaly before stepping forward again. As her fingers near the faucet, a sudden loud swoosh sends a splash of warm water onto her face.

"Oooh!" she exclaims, startled. Eyes wide open, she watches as the two streams of water rise before her, twining around each other like helices, climbing high, and cascading back down towards her.

Instinctively, she raises her hands to shield her face, but the streams distort into forceful jets aimed at the windows, crashing against the glass with the roar of unleashed rivers.

Looking at her hands, Nysa stiffens, her eyes wide. "Is it me?" she whispers, her voice a mixture of awe and uncertainty. "Am I doing this?"

Her gaze fixed on her fingers, she tentatively raises her hand towards the jet of water. As if responding to her command, the stream gracefully ascends, arching towards the ceiling.

"Should I...?" she murmurs, her voice trailing off as she wrestles with her disbelief and the thrilling possibility of control. With a swift, deliberate movement, she brings her hand down. The water obeys, morphing into millions of tiny droplets that shower down upon her. Laughter erupts from her, a sound mingled with shock and delight.

As the water dances around her, Nysa experiments with her movements, her arms weaving through the air, guiding the fluid streams with a newfound grace. With a sharp gesture, she directs the water back to the floor, her movements becoming more confident with each pass.

Kneeling, she scoops up the water, feeling a release in her chest—an untying of the knots of fear and doubt. She stands, turns towards the mirror, and sees her reflection smiling back through the droplets that speckled the glass.

Feeling lighter, Nysa approaches the door, a playful smirk playing on her lips. With a dramatic flourish, she flings her hands upward, commanding the water to rise and gather.

The droplets coalesce into a shimmering sentence floating in the air:

What forces can one command when one sees?

A warm buzz fills her belly, her eyes lock on the glistening message. A moment passes in silent wonder.

"Me? Command forces?" she ponders aloud, her shoulders tensing as she exhales deeply. Letting her gaze fall, she watches the sentence dissolve into a cascade of water, returning to the floor with a gentle splash.

Grabbing her phone, Nysa quickly types a message:

```
 Maisha, can I see you? I need to talk, can
I come now?
```

The reply is swift:

```
Of course. Meet me at my place.
```

14.

Cups on the table and a teapot steaming, Maisha sits in her living room, a serene figure awaiting her guest. She watches with a hint of amusement as Nysa hurries in, her presence a stark contrast to the calm of the morning.

"Take your time," Maisha chuckles as Nysa, sweating and breathless, frantically tosses her purse onto a chair.

Hands on her knees, bent forward, the young woman catches her breath. "Huff, I am... drained..." she manages to say between jagged breaths.

"Why the rush, Nysa? Sit, drink your rooibos. When you finish, let's go for a walk," Maisha suggests gently, her voice grounding.

Raising an eyebrow, Nysa stares at Maisha for a moment before complying. As she sits and takes the cup, she savors the quietude, the scent, and the warmth of the rooibos soothing her.

Her breath slowing, Nysa turns to Maisha. "I have so much to tell you, Maisha. Things have been happening... I don't even know how... I mean..." She trails off, shakes her head, and exhales deeply. "You wouldn't believe me even if I swore..."

Maisha smiles quietly, her eyes closing as she nods slightly. "Dear," she begins, her smile lingering as she tilts her head, "there's just something about being an old lady..." She opens her eyes and takes a seat opposite Nysa. "Drink, child. And let's get some fresh air."

Finishing her cup, Nysa silently welcomes the warmth and peace. She leans back in her chair, loosening her shoes with a heel strike, a contented sigh escaping her lips.

In a companionable silence, they both sit for a moment longer, eyes closed. They open their eyes almost simultaneously, rise from their chairs, and take each other's hands.

Nysa, her mind still wandering, tucks a bag of jelly candies on the table, grabs her purse, and they both pick up a bottle at the entrance before leaving. As they make their way through the bustling city—cars honking, babies crying—Maisha turns to Nysa, her voice breaking the silence.

"How pleasant it is to wander in the city," she muses softly. "I don't know if I ever told you about him, Nysa, but it reminds me of my father. A very special man. Years ago, I used to walk around the city just like we do today, with him."
A tender smile touches Maisha's lips as they walk.
"You don't talk much about him," Nysa remarks softly, keeping her eyes on the ground.

"He was exceptionally wise, possessing knowledge that seemed to belong only to the past," Maisha begins, her voice taking on the cadence of a storyteller as they slow their pace. "His ancestors were part of a tribe of elders who lived in harmony with nature, their wisdom passed down through spoken words and tales. As a boy, my father would listen for hours to the ancient knowledge shared in stories, and I, in turn, grew up listening to these stories through him."

Nysa glances at Maisha, curiosity piqued by the description of such a lineage. "At that time, elders would scar their skins," Maisha continues. "Women did so to protect themselves and their daughters from assault, and men marked themselves as trophies of their successes in battle. Because their scars were always visible, never hidden, other tribes called them 'The Marked Ones'."

Nysa stops walking, a knot forming in her stomach. "The Marked Ones?"

"Yes," Maisha nods, her smile gentle. "They were believed to possess great power, fueled by their center of convergence—an old battlefield where smoky vapors bridged the present with the spirits of ancestors, and where countless rocks stood as monuments to their legacy."

As Maisha speaks, Nysa's finger traces an unconscious path along her forearm, her mind flashing with faint memories of an ancient arena, smoky vapors, old rocks, and a child with yellow eyes. Her fingers tighten on Maisha's arm. "What is this place, Maisha? What does this all mean?"

"My father called it a Muse," Maisha explains, her voice dropping to a whisper. "He believed it spoke to him, that they were connected. The smoke, he said, was the whispers of their ancestors. To me, it looked nothing more than empty ruins—a bit creepy for a little girl. But to him, to The Marked Ones, it was something more, visible only to certain eyes."

"Maisha, these vapors..." Nysa hugs herself, shivering slightly.

Maisha meets her gaze in silence, a profound understanding in her eyes. "I don't know... Would I be crazy to think that I might be..."

Nysa's hand rises to her forehead as she leans forward, swaying gently. Her other hand reaches out, seeking Maisha's support.

"You're alright, child," Maisha murmurs soothingly. "What do we truly know of the weights we carry?"

Breathing deeply, Nysa steadies herself and meets Maisha's gaze again. "I need... air. Would you take me to The Center?" she whispers, pressing the lady's arm for support.

"Nysa. I think that you should not. Not like that. Let me drive you home, or to the park."

Abruptly, Nysa withdraws her hand and pushes away Maisha's.
"No! You don't get to decide! You don't understand. Leave me. I prefer to go alone."
She turns her back and runs towards the Liapsar Boulevard.

15.

Moments later
6:47 PM – The Center

"I need... to see him," Nysa mutters under her breath as she rushes through the corridors of the first floor. Her head spins with urgency, her eyes darting from face to face, turning corners with a frantic pace.

Every person she passes is not the one she seeks.

"I need to see Thorne. Has anyone seen Thorne?" she asks aloud, desperation edging into her voice.

"Professor, are you well?" A concerned voice cuts through her thoughts. Alistair, one of her students. "He taught a class upstairs this morning, but... Would you like to sit, Professor? You look unwell."

Pausing, Nysa fixes her gaze on the young man's concerned face. "Alistair. Remember that sloppy grand rond de jambe you did at your midterms? Do you want to pass? Take me to the fourth floor."

Moments later, the elevator dings open onto a quiet fourth floor. She steps out, energized by a sudden resolve, shaking her arms and shoulders loose. Nysa peers into each room along the corridor—chin up, head extended, tiptoeing for a better view. Each glance sharpens the knot in her stomach.

Left... Right, room 4-108... Left, room 4-109... Right, room 4-110... Left...

Finally, room 4-202.

"No. I missed him," she sighs, with heaviness.

She enters the studio—her studio—and walks over to the bright window. Sliding down to the floor, Nysa lets her gaze settle on the sun outside, its brightness contrasts with the chill seeping into her bones.

The city buzzes beneath her—a living, breathing entity of its own. She wraps her arms around her knees, allowing herself a rare moment of peace. Here, alone with her thoughts, she views the world from above, yet unseen by the world itself.

As she soaks in the solitude, a familiar voice breaks the silence.

"Knock knock. Nysa, it's me."

Her heart skips as she turns to face the door, her mind racing with anticipation and a flurry of emotions.

Nysa stands up and dusts off her skirt. "Come in, Mr. Wolehead."

"How are you, Nysa? I haven't seen you around these past days," his tone is with genuine concern.

She remains silent, fingers twisting.

"Alistair was worried about you. He came to see me. I must admit, I am worried too. You've been missing classes, isolating yourself...
How are you, truly?" he presses gently.

A slow breath escapes her as she meets his gaze. Her lips part to speak, but he interrupts. "Would you like to take some rest, while another professor covers your classes?"

Her response is cut off as tears well up, blurring her vision. "Oh, Nysa. You must be under a lot of stress," he says softly, touching her shoulder gently.

Her body tenses under his touch, and a tear trickles down her cheek. She nods mutely in agreement.

"Consider it done. Finn will cover for you. I hope we can have our old Nysa back soon," he says warmly, removing his hand and walking towards the door. Before leaving, he pauses, "By the way, Nysa, are you cold? You're wearing your jacket with this heat."

His question lingers unanswered as she stares blankly at him. Once alone, she faces the window and tries to unzip her jacket, but the zipper jams. Frustration surges as she tugs harder, but it refuses to budge.

Desperately, she attempts to pull the jacket off over her head, but it clings to her, tightening around her arms as if alive. Her heart races, breaths come in short bursts. She wrestles with the fabric, her movements growing frantic as it constricts further.

She pauses, breath held, hoping The Jacket will loosen.

Breathe, Nysa. Just breathe. Remember 'what does not break you...'

The fabric creases and wraps around her arms. Clenching her fists, she hits, strikes, punches on her sleeves, pulls them up and down in vain.

And, with a sudden click, the zipper gives way, sliding all the way up to her neck by itself. Wordless, drained, she leans against the window, her fists pounding against the glass in futile desperation. One, two, ten strikes, each one leaving her more exhausted, her fingers numbing with pain.

Warm, red tears stream down her face as she finally turns away, stumbling out of the room towards the bathroom, seeking refuge in its solitude.

16.

In the bathroom's dim light, the water feels neither warm nor cold. It carries a chill that seeps into her bones. Nysa exhales, her breath mingling with the cold air, her voice a whisper. "Just... dull. And freezing."

Seated on the floor, her legs sprawled out, she leans forward, letting her forehead rest painfully against her bony knee. As her eyes shut, a white cloud of emptiness envelops her mind, filling her thoughts with a heavy, numbing fog. Her head sways gently—left, right, down—in a slow, almost rhythmic dance of despair.

Her arms fall limply by her sides, fingers tapping the wet floor, sending tiny, filthy splashes against her leggings. Each tap, draining what little energy remains within her, her life force ebbing into the cold tile.

As her pulse slows, the smoky fog in her head begins to dissolve, her facial muscles relaxing into a profound nothingness. She remains there, a figure of stillness, as time stretches and thins around her.

.

.

Time passes.

Memories start arising in her mind:

A young girl, skinny and dressed in a school uniform, sits on the stairwell steps of what seems like a school library, examining her arms. Her sleeves are rolled up, revealing forearms encircled by tiny dots. With furrowed brows and lips bitten in concentration, she traces circles around the marks.

The sun's rays dim, the vision blurring and then sharpening again. Now, the same girl sits on a park bench, gazing across a silent body of water. She lifts her head to squint at the sun, and turns as a shadow approaches—a woman, neither tall nor wide, with a small, silver rock pendant glinting at her neck.

"Can I sit, child?" The woman's voice gently breaks through the haze.

The girl nods quietly, her gaze fixed on the woman beside her.

"What is your name, young girl?"
Silence.
"Mine is Maisha."
More silence.
"Do you like animals?"

The girl remains silent, her eyes never leaving the woman.

"You like dogs, maybe?"
Silence again.
"Here, this one is for you, if you want it."

She hands the girl a stuffed dog, soft and cottony.

"Am I not too old for a stuffed toy?"
 "I think you are just old enough."

The girl accepts the gift with a quiet thanks. The sunrays fade, and the figures of her and the lady dissolve into nothingness.

The cloud in Nysa's mind forms and vanishes. Her ears pick up a distant sound of aspiration.

Roaring.
Louder.
Closer.

Like a vacuum cleaner?

She squints against the sunset light filtering in through a window, hearing it again. *The cleaning team? Am I... at The Center? Oh, yes!*

She snaps back to reality, rubs her eyes, and slaps her cheeks. "Wake up, Nysa!" she mutters to herself. "Get up!"

She plunges her hands into the puddle around her, pushes down on her wrists, and shifts to her right side. Knees on the floor, she straightens her back, grasps the handle of the toilet cabinet above, and pulls herself up with a groan.

"My last class!" she exclaims as the vapors in her head clear. "8:06 PM. Hurry, Nysa!"

She halts at the door, noting her dirt-covered outfit.

"24 minutes left. Shower. Change. Teach.
Can you do it?" she whispers, staring at her reflection in the mirror. "Of course, you can."

She dashes into a shower cabin, letting the lukewarm water cascade over her, loosening her muscles, settling the hairs on her neck.

"8:24 PM." Towel. Cream. Locker.
She changes into a black V-neck sleeveless bodysuit and nude open-toe heels. A glance in the mirror, a swipe of Glastonbury matte lipstick. "Camouflage the carnage..."

With her palms on the sink, arms straight, she stares into her eyes. "Breathe in, Nysa. And out. And in. Come on. You can do it." She feels her shoulders sag with each breath. "You can do it, Nysa. Of course... You can."

One last look at the water where she had sat on the floor, she sighs, turns, and heads out of the bathroom towards room 4-202.

Nysa bursts into the studio, her voice carrying ahead of her. "Guuuyyy..." She halts mid-step, her shout trailing off into a stunned silence as she surveys the room. "...ys!" The studio is unusually quiet, all 40 students' eyes fixed on her, a sea of expectancy.

Frowning, she scans their faces. "Okay, what's the catch? It's 8:30 PM, no shouting, no complaints, no... noise? What's happening?"

"We heard, Professor," one student begins, the others nodding in agreement. "This is our last class with you for the semester."

"Yes, we heard Professor Finn will be teaching us from tomorrow. So, we all came..."

A tender smile breaks across Nysa's face as she clears her throat, touched. "Thank you, guys. I really appreciate it. Sincerely."

"We appreciate you, too, Professor." The room fills with a soft murmur of agreement.

Silently, she moves to the center of the room, her voice steady but soft. "I propose, since this is our last class, to review our salsa routine. Spread out, please." She clips on her microphone, grabs the remote control, and presses play. "And let's begin with our shines! Ready? From the top!"

As the music fills the room, the energy shifts palpably:

"Okay, let's go through it one more time, and we'll add our last part."

"That's it, yes, you got it! Yes, ladies, point your feet, remember your styling!"

"Okay, guys, moving on! Let's add our last piece." She turns off the music and partners up with a male student.

"Watch, guys. Right after the kick here, turn, and prep..." A sharp pain interrupts her as her ankle twists again. "No, I'm fine! Keep going! Lori, please, with Daniel, come here! You'll show us."

They demonstrate flawlessly: "From the kick, and... Kick, turn, prep, triple turn, yes! And..."

"Excellent! Guys, looking clean!!" The music ends.

"Okay, guys! We're done for today! Please take all your stuff, put the chairs back, and don't forget anything. Professor Finn is a great teacher, highly technical. Take advantage, and learn!"

As she finishes, the room bursts into applause. A smile stretches across her face, her ankle tingling, a burning sensation creeping up her forearm as she watches the 40 students circle her with smiles and claps.

"Thank you so much, guys," she responds, her voice warm with genuine appreciation.

Seated, she waves goodbye, the studio slowly emptying to the endless stream of thanks, compliments, and expressions of gratitude.

The voices fade into far-off sounds.

And finally—silence.

"See... you made it, Nysa," she mutters through clenched teeth.

Sliding off her chair to the floor, she lets her head fall back, her throat open, and exhales a loud, deep sigh. Her gaze fixes on her forearm, brushing the scars with her finger, feeling every texture and memory they carry.

"They were called 'The Marked Ones.' " Maisha's voice echoes in her ears.

Slowly, Nysa pushes herself up and tentatively places half her weight on her ankle. She groans under the strain. Gradually, she adds more weight, her face contorting with each shift. Eventually, a satisfied grin breaks through the pain. She counts to three and lets her weight drop back onto the chair. Her head falls back, her mouth opens wide, and a scream tears through the silence of the night.

Meanwhile, the pain is excruciating for him as well. His knees nearly buckle under the agony. Another stifled scream escapes as the marks on his forearm burst into flames. He clutches his arms tightly—a thunderclap resonates.

He inhales sharply; she exhales slowly. He pushes up from the floor, struggling to his knees and nearly collapsing again as lightning strikes once more. Barely standing, he steadies himself long enough to see her through the laminated glass door of room 4-202.

Inside, the room is empty. Nysa lowers her head, and the tingling subsides. No more burning, no more pain. Her jaw relaxes, her eyes cease their twitching. Around her, there are no lights, no music, only darkness.

The door opens to a silent shadow. Watching her. Standing still. *Is it real?*

She turns back to the mirror, her eyes meeting the glowing yellow ones reflected there. She breathes quietly, her blood pounding in her ears. Slowly, she lifts her arm, clenches her fist, and—*Crack.* Something breaks.

The mirror, as if screaming, shatters into countless pieces.

She raises her arms, elbows guarding her face against the flying shards. Yet, she remains soundless. In front of her, a shard hangs suspended, sharp and menacing.

Her fingers tentatively reach out, touching the icy shard. The cold numbs her fingertips, sending shivers down her spine. The shard edges closer to her chest. Her gaze hollow, her jaw clenched, a tear traced down her cheek.

Her fingers wrap around the shard, pressing it against her chest, then sliding it down to her wrist, tracing the haunting marks. Until—a drop of blood forms. *Don't do this,* he murmurs from behind the door.

The drop glistens on the shard, mirrored in her eyes. Her chest rises slowly, the single drop becoming a steady stream. *This is all my fault. How could I give up on myself, on my body? Let myself reach this low?* And the shadow around her grows, expands.

—and envelops her entirely.

IV.

*"What is chosen when all paths
open?"*

17.

That same night
11:26 PM – Somewhere...

Nysa stands in the center of a room, draped in a white layered tulle knee dress. Moonlight bathes her face, lending a surreal glow to the otherwise dark space. She examines her attire with a frown. "Where am I?"

Lifting her gaze to the ceiling, she spins slowly, her eyes scanning the surroundings. Darkness envelops her, but for the grandeur of The Center's performance theater and its magnificent crystal tiered chandelier. Millions of tiny, glimmering glass squares shimmer, casting reflections on the framed pictures of past professors adorning the walls.

She squints, feeling the overwhelming presence of someone else.

Thorne stands across the room, clad in a black suit with a striped sleeve shirt, his face radiant under the moonlight. He steps toward her, bending slightly to offer his hand, his presence as mesmerizing as the crystals above.

A dance begins to form in the silence between them.

"Where are we? Am I dreaming?" Nysa asks, her voice a whisper lost in the vastness of the theater.

He smiles gently, his eyes holding hers. "Where do you think we are?"

"At The Center?" she ventures.

"Well... there you go" he replies.
Feeling her gaze on him, his smile fades. His voice softens: "You cut yourself, Nysa. You are not safe. Not yet. We are somewhere between two worlds. Until you make a decision."

His gaze lowers to his hand and back to her. "I assure you, it will not break from a firm handshake."

A chill runs down her spine. She scans the room once more, and with a resigned sigh, she grasps his offered hand. A cold shiver accompanies the contact.

Instantly, she finds herself drawn closer to him, her eyes locked with his. At the temples, her pulse stalls momentarily—then races.

"My hand was not offered for a handshake, but rather, for you to catch," he murmurs, his breath a warm breeze against her ear.

Her eyes flicker downwards, but as the piano in the background begins to play, her heel slips off and clatters to the floor. Her right foot, as if of its own accord, rises into the air.

A wide smile spreads across her face, and she places her free hand on his shoulder, surrendering to the dance that is about to unfold.

Warm. Hot.

Burning.

Nysa raises her head, her gaze locking with Thorne's, feeling the quickening pulse on his neck. In an almost imperceptible motion, he spins her, his jacket shimmering and vanishing. Sleeveless now, the marks on his arms are exposed as he fixes his intense gaze on her.

She looks to the floor, perplexed—nothing. Everything faded as if into thin air. "How is this..." she starts, but silence chokes her words.

Their eyes remain locked, her breath halts, her blinking pauses. The clinking of the chandelier and the notes of the piano freeze. The pressure of her palm on his shoulder intensifies.

Her stomach unravels.

He lifts her in a spin, the smile on her face widening with the moment. He smiles back and releases her hand.

Her arm falls to her lap, heavy. She blinks, hesitates, her shoulders sagging under a sudden weight. He turns away, and she reaches out, tapping his shoulder, straightening her back as she extends her arm.

"Mine either will not break from a solid handshake," she declares.

Slowly, Thorne turns back to her, locking eyes once again. His hand captures hers, pressing it against her heart, holding it there in a profound silence that stretches between them.

He guides her back to the dance floor. Lifting her, her arms reach out and down to his shoulders. As she slides down slowly, her eyes never leave his, her lips tingling, drawn to his.

Heart pounding, his arms heavy yet steady as they support her, he freezes, holds the gaze. His lips, burning with an unseen fire, inch closer to hers.

His jaw clenches. "She is so close... too close..." his mind whispers.

Images flood his mind—him as a young child clutching his knees, his parents in the distance, arguing, ragged breaths escaping, rain pouring during a thunderous dance.

His arms tremble as thunderclaps resonate outside. Nysa startles, tapping on his shoulders.

"No!!" He shakes his head forcefully, setting her gently back onto the floor. He drops her hand, turns his back.

His retinas sting from the image of his childhood, thunderstorms raging in his eyes.

"You are still too fragile for me," he murmurs, his voice a blend of regret and resolve.

He turns back, his gaze downward, leaving her in the quiet aftermath of what almost was.

Her lungs hold her breath, her stomach takes a hit. A tear escapes her eye, quickly wiped away.

"Fragile?" she pauses, frozen. He meets her gaze, silent and intense.

"Who do you think you are to…" she begins, her voice trembling with emotion.

He steps towards her, capturing her frantic arm, raising an eyebrow in challenge.

"Who do I think I am?" he retorts with a smirk. "I'd say, who do you think YOU are, Nysa, to come after me?"

His hand still pressing on her arm, he slides his fingers down to hers, leading her back to the center of the stage. "Let's see if you can dance as much as you can talk."

With a frown and raised eyebrow, she returns his look. A threatening gaze meets his, her chin up, she smirks back. She kneels to remove her remaining heel and tosses it off the stage. He pulls her close against him; his grip is tight, his breath loud against her neck.

The dance intensifies—pulling, pushing, bending, hopping, sliding, spinning. Her heart pounds fiercely in her chest. Her bare feet scratch the floor; her mouth opens for air as the beat quickens, blood rushing in her ears.

She tugs at his arms, he resists; she pulls again. Her hand slaps his forearm, his fingers tighten on her wrist.

She pulls, slaps, crushes his dance shoes, and yanks harder. He holds on, then releases abruptly, contracting his chest, locking eyes with her once more.

She meets his stare, holding it for a charged moment before breaking away.

The tension in her temples builds, a boiling rage in her stomach, and she exits the stage and grabs her shoe. Sitting down, she begins to lace it.

Watching her silently, he takes a step forward. "You are strong," he states simply.
And adds: "I know that you are not well. But you are still standing. You chose to grab my hand. You chose to live."

She looks up at him, her expression unreadable. He kneels, takes the lace, and finishes tying her shoe. Gently, he helps her to her feet.

He looks down into her face, then at her lips, his gaze intense. She holds his stare, thunder rolling in her eyes.

"I don't get you," she breathes out.

"You don't have to," he replies with a smirk, the room thick with unsaid words.

"I get you. I might even…" she starts, a deep breath catching in her throat, her heart pounding.

"Love…"

She quickly shakes her head, a chill running down her spine.

She grabs the soiled train of her dress and limps out of the room, one shoe on, her ribs shaking with suppressed emotions.

18.

That same night
2:57 AM – Destination: 610 Greenhole Square

In the taxi, heading to her apartment, Nysa's heart slows. Eyes closed, head spinning and aching, she runs her index finger over the white, cotton crepe bandage on her arm—a reminder of where the shard cut her. Blurry images flicker through her mind: Thorne lacing her shoe, wrapping her forearm in warm cotton, a voice whispering the L-word. Whose voice was it? "Was any of this real?" she wonders aloud, shaking her head and relaxing back against the car seat.

The taxi stops, and she mechanically makes her way to the elevator. Sixth floor. She enters her apartment, drops her keys, sheds her jacket, and collapses into bed, grabbing the comforting plush of the ear-shaped pillow. The lights go out; she's still in her clothes as she pulls the heavy, freshly scented merino wool blanket over her face. She closes her eyes, breathes deeply, and steadies herself.

I'm back in that dark corridor, facing the cracked and ominously dark mirror. To my right, the child appears, frail, ribs visible under their shirt. "Why did you come back?" the child's voice echoes again.

"Where are we? Who are you?"

"How could you forget...?" The child's breath smells faintly of decay, their figure glowing in the dark before vanishing.

Jolted awake, Nysa finds her T-shirt sticking to her sweat-dampened back. Her pulse races.
"Forget? What?" she gasps, feeling a fleeting tingle on her forearms that quickly disappears.

Now awake, she throws off the blanket and grabs the water bottle from her nightstand. She takes three slow sips, three more, whispering to herself, "Calm down, heart. We're safe." She slices a white, rectangular pill in half on the table and swallows it, then inserts her foam earplugs.

Selecting a playlist on her phone, she chooses "432Hz Calm your mind" from Spotify. The soothing tones calm her. She massages her temples, takes a few deep breaths, and lets herself sink into the mattress. Gradually, her mind numbs, and she drifts into a deep, dreamless sleep.

When she wakes, her mind is calm, but her heart pounds at the memory of her dance with Thorne. She hadn't wanted to let him in, but it was too late. *If I don't put an end to this now, I might never be able to push him away.*

19.

The next morning
7:03 AM – A park nearby

"I don't even know what you're doing right now..."
Her hands rest on her chest, one crossed over the other, as she mutters to herself.
"And would you slow down when I speak to you?" she scolds, slapping the space above her pounding heart.

Resigned, she lowers her hands and sighs.

The early morning park feels like a balm. The city's green lung, still quiet before the storm, welcomes her. She walks to her usual bench beneath a leafy pine and sits facing the still, reflective water.

Timid sunrays kiss her arms—along with the tiny dots that still linger there.

"He wears them too... uncovered..." she murmurs, flashes of their dance flickering in her mind. His bare forearms. His glowing face. That smile.

Her fingers brush the bumpy, scarred skin, and a shiver runs through her.
She rolls her shoulders back and inhales deeply, her body basking in the gentle warmth of the waking sun.

Turning her head, she smiles at the sky, squinting, blinking into the light.

Her mind untangles. Her breath deepens.
 The tingling in her fingers returns, and her eyelids soften. Every inch of her fills with a kind of energy only The Sun can deliver. Silently, she offers thanks to this constant, faithful companion in the sky.

Leaning back against the wooden bench, she exhales.
 A fresh breeze glides across her shoulder. A subtle scent—wood, spice—brushes past her nose.
 His.

Her eyes scan the park. Right. Left. Forward.
 She smiles. Then erases it.

"What is it that you feel?" she asks her heart, pressing her hands against it again.
 "Tell me—do we hate him?
 ...or do we *not* hate him?"

Another breeze brushes her cheek.
 "Okay, it's getting cold. Time to go."

She stands, hoists her hobo bag onto her shoulder, and takes a few steps toward the water—

Cling.

She turns. Something dropped on the bench?
 Shielding her eyes with one hand, she squints. Her other arm reaches out instinctively—
 A die.

A single six-sided die, worn and weathered, its numbers faded.

"Warm?"
She curls her fingers around it. Opens them again.
Not warm.
Hot.

Turning in every direction, she surveys the quiet park and the water.
 No one.

She frowns, places the die back on the bench, and steps away.
 It stays. Still. Silent. Inanimate.

She walks back, picks it up again, cups it in her palm, rolls it once—and clenches her fist around it.
 Slides it into her pocket.

One last look at the bench. She turns and walks off.

A billboard overhead catches her eye:

What does one face in being?

The words stretch across the sky in bold white letters.

"Another cryptic sentence?" she mutters.
She rolls her eyes. "Enough now. With the craziness."

Pulling out her phone, she snaps a picture of the ad.
Selects the words: "What does one face in being..."
Search.

```
...Google searching...
 Results found: 0.
```

Unbothered, she saves the image and pockets her phone.
 Crossing the street, she bumps shoulders with a young
man.
 "Sorry!" she calls back—
—and hurries towards home.

20.

Back home, she powers on her laptop and reaches for her phone.

```
"Maisha, I am so sorry for the other day.
For pushing you away. Please call me back.
I'd like to hear the rest of the story
about your dad. Please… call me when you
get this."
```

Her pulse pounds at her neck as she opens the search bar. Fingers race across the keyboard.

Google.
 "Let's try again: *What does one face in being?'*"
She hovers over the *Enter* key…
"No. Let's add: *'Cryptic messages'.*"

Results found: 0.

She exhales through her teeth.
"Okay. Let's try… *'The Marked Ones'.*"

Results found: 9,847:

"Paranormal activity… No.
 Religious cults… No.
No… No…"

She sighs, deeper this time. "Still nothing on her dad's tribe."

Phone again. Maisha. Call.

Voicemail.

She groans. "Why isn't she answering? Is she still upset with me?"

Pacing, she taps her foot hard against the floor. Circles the room. Her breath shortens, quickens.

"None of this makes any sense!"

She throws herself onto the sofa and flips open Netflix. Scrolls. Clicks. *Play.*
Scratches her head. Bites her lip.
Pause.
Exit.
Power off.

"Okay. That's enough."

She shuts the laptop and stands abruptly, her hands shaking. Her leg bounces uncontrollably.

"I'm done with all this. I'm done with this..."
She grabs her phone and hurls it across the room,
"...city!"

Jacket. Door. Slam.
Down the stairs. Out into the street.

She walks, mind blank. Each step is faster.
 And faster.

The sounds of the city swell around her—honking, yelling, grinding gears—but none of it reaches her. Her breath comes sharper as the city's stench—smoke and metal and chemicals—burns her nose.

Faster.
 She nearly runs.

The wind lashes at her face, slicing her breath into clouds. Her eyes sting. Tears escape and race down her cheeks—she swipes them away with the back of her hand.

Her pulse pounds, pounding—
 Up her neck, into her skull.

Heat rushes from her legs to her chest, rising to her temples. She slows, wipes her running nose, and gasps for air.

One hand finds a wall. She bends forward, bracing herself, panting. Her lungs blaze.
 She unzips her jacket, falls back against the wall, and slides down to the ground.

The freezing air does nothing to cool the fire raging inside her body.
 Sweat runs down her spine.

She peels off her jacket—burning.
Her vision spins.
Her right eye dims—
Black specks first,
Then splashes, like spilled ink.

Still sitting, she reaches out blindly, arm flailing for help.
Her head spins again—
And drops.
The world goes dark.

She opens her eyes, startled by the cacophony around her.
Movement. Shouts. Crying.
Footsteps rushing past.
Overhead lights blur into a buzz.
Bips! and *buzzz!*
Echo sharply in the sterile air.

An ECG scanner beeps steadily.
Blood pressure monitors pulse beside her.
Oxygen tubes. A needle in her arm.

I'm at the hospital.

A jolt—someone begins rolling her trolley through the corridor.

"Ma'am, are you awake?"
"Ma'am, don't close your eyes."

The gurney turns. They pass under flickering lights, into a darker hallway.

"Ma'am, we're going to do a quick scan."
"Ma'am, do not close your eyes."
"Ma'am, can you hear me?"

"Ma'aaaaaaaam..."

Her vision blurs. Her eyelids weigh tons.

I feel my eyes closing...

In the hazy reflection of a nearby monitor, letters flicker—

What calls one elsewhere?

I feel my eyes closing...

Her hand, weak, dips into her jacket pocket.
 Her fingers find the dice.
 Rolling it gently.

Her head tips backward

—and just like that,
 she's back.

There.

21.

Moments later
At The Ancient Place...

"Don't turn to The Sun and its warmth to save you.
 It's just me and you now..."
I hear.

And—
The bone-wracking dance of pain inside me begins.

And—
 I collapse.

I've always believed human life is a gift.
  That we're each here to bring something—*something unique*—to others, or to the world.
  Something shaped by what makes us different.

When my genes were forming, there was one in particular that refused to fit the mold.
 It happens to many of us in different ways.
 You might have something in you, too—something that refuses to conform.
 In that sense, from birth, we're all rebels.

For me, it was the gene responsible for producing hemoglobin—the protein that carries oxygen in the blood.
What is it for you?
That thing you despise? That makes you feel different?
Or even... unworthy?

My red blood cells aren't round and smooth like they should be.
They're twisted. Deformed.
Sickle-shaped.
When they circulate, they scrape. Get stuck in vessels.
Clot together.
They block blood flow, starving my organs of oxygen.

It's called sickle cell disease (SCD).

Growing up, having SCD was like being a secret agent—living a double life.
There was the *real* world: friends, school, pop songs, homework, grades.
And then, the secret world:
Painful crises.
Ambulances.
Oxygen masks.
Transfusions.
Needle pricks.
Darkness.

This second world, though invisible, always left visible marks.

In my case, it starts with yellow eyes.
Stress. Fatigue. Fear of the cold.
Scars on my skin.
Bones that feel like they'll snap in half.

And in those moments, I doubt everything I've believed.
Is life really a gift?
Is this *really* worth it?

Honestly?
I'm tired.
I don't have the energy for another toll to pay.

To feel *less*.
To watch my confidence dissolve.
To be reminded that I'm *different*.
To feel like I don't belong in this world.

I hate how vulnerable it makes me feel.
I've spent my life trying to be tough.
I had to be.

Like the day, twenty years ago.
We were playing, running, shouting in the neighborhood.
Later that day, I fell in the shower.
That's when I had my first cerebrovascular accident.
A stroke.

What was it for you, dear reader?

What childhood moment still defines the way you survive?

Since I was young, I developed a strategy:
When I reach the edge of pain, I disconnect.
My mind does it alone. It goes blank.
My spirit rises.
Floats above my body.
Above the world.
It returns only when it's safe again.
Safe to live *inside* this body.

But this time...

I don't know.
When is *one more* too many?

I hesitate.

They say, *"What doesn't kill you makes you stronger."*
It's been my mantra since I was six.
Maybe you have one too?

Some long-held belief—probably false—that has imprisoned you.

I never questioned mine.
It was born the same day the pain and shame began.
Hospital crises.
Agony.

And, you know... Loss. Grief. Traumas.
All the devastating, soul-breaking events life throws at us.

But now... I'm not so sure.

Is it true?
 Do I need to keep surviving more pain, over and over, to
be "strong"?

I...
 I don't know.

God crosses my mind again.

I am tempted—
 to give up.

Maybe I should
 just
 close
 my
 eyes.

I do. Gently. Slowly.

And then—
 I think...
 I see her?

My name is Maisha.

And I made a promise.
 More than that—a vow.
 Never to interfere.

But I also have a duty.

To protect her.

The promise, or the duty?
 I don't know which matters more.
 But this much is certain—
 I will act.

I feel the fire rising—
 first in my eyes, then in my arms,
 then my hands.

I run.

The stones scrape at my ankles.
 My feet—raw, burning.
 Still, I push forward.

Faster.

I throw my arms into the air, destroying everything in my
path.
 Tree bark. Stones. Walls.
 They shatter.

My hands spin, gathering force, as smoke and dust blind my sight,
 sting my lungs.

Still—onward.

And, I see her.
 Curled on the ground. Shrunken.
 Giving up.

My breath stumbles.
 My hands erupt again, blasting toward the wall ahead.
 I drop down, crash beside her, and press my fingers to her neck.

Her pulse—faint. So faint.

I lift her head into my lap.
 Her arms—marked. Bright red.

I look up.

The wall stares back at me, cloaked in smoke.
 Unmoving. Unfeeling.

"ENOUGH!" I scream.
 Electricity rips from my hands.
 One hand. Then both.

My fury sears through my eyes.
I glance back—
Her pulse wanes.

Gently, I lower her.
And stand.

I face the wall.
It. Me.

"I SAID ENOUGH!"

Lightning explodes from my palms.
The wall trembles—barely.
It feeds on my rage.
And throws it back.

I dig my feet into the ground and strike again.

This time, a bolt slices through the smoke.
A fracture. Small, but there.

I squint through the heat.
Another shock. The wall cracks.
The smoke thickens.

"Everything has a price," it growls.

The earth shakes.
Stone explodes.

I extend my leg toward her.
 The stones shift. Fall away.
 Her body lifts.

She levitates. Safe.

Blinded by smoke, I hold my breath.
 Keep my arms raised.

Fire blazes in my palm.
 I hurl it—
once.
 Twice.
 Three times.

The wall shakes—but still stands.

I look back.
 She breathes. Barely.

I turn forward again, baring my teeth.
 "WATCH US."

My hands burn.
 My foot strikes the ground.
 Cracks ripple outward.
 Rocks rise and collapse.
 Thunder screams across the sky.

The ground splits.
 The wall lets out a groan—deep, guttural.

And then—

Rain.

A downpour.
 Smoke vanishes.

The wall—fractured, scarred—breaks.
 Crumbles.
 Falls.

A roar of stone crashing to earth.

I drop to my knees.
 My arms fall limp.
 My lungs finally release.

I look at her.
 She lowers gently to the ground.
 Her chest rises.

A pulse.

I rise.
 I wave.

And as I walk forward,
 a glimmering net wraps around her—
 lifts her—
 and follows my lead.

22.

The next day
4:38 PM – 7 RedBricks Avenue

"I survived.
And I am okay.

Not physically—my body is a wreck.
I spent the night bleeding.
But I got some rest.

Mentally... I feel strong.
Stronger than I've felt in a long time.
I think I can fight.

I don't know yet what I'm fighting *for*—
...but I know where to begin.

My class. My students.
I'll fight for what's mine.

There's no turning back now.

...I think."

Carefully, she fastens the bandages around her legs and stomach. Pants on, jacket zipped, she grabs her small bottle of liquid and steps out, heading toward Maisha's room.

Knock knock.
 No answer.

She presses her ear to the door again—silence.
 "Maisha? Maisha, are you here?"

Her brows lift. She tilts her head, sniffs the air.
 "...No hot vanilla smell today?"

Knock knock.
 A little firmer this time.

"Maisha?"

Behind the door, a tremor. A voice she can't hear:
"I hear you, child. I hear you.
 But I cannot respond. Please, go.
 No broken vow shall be left unpunished."

One last knock. A sigh.
 Nysa tiptoes to the living room, walks over to the desk.

"I don't know what you did, or how, but I know you saved me... Thank you."
 She scribbles the note and leaves it on the table, pressing it down with the bottle of liquid.

She turns and leaves—heading straight to The Center.

Knock knock.
 "May I speak with you, Mister Wolehead?"

"Nysa! Oh dear God, what are you doing here?"

He stands abruptly, circles his desk to face her.

"I thought you were unwell. You still look a bit..."
She arches an eyebrow. He clears his throat.
"...fatigued?"

"I'm better now, Mister Wolehead. I'll continue to rest and care for myself...
But I need my class back. I need to teach again."

He watches her. Silent. One step closer.

"I mean—want to teach again. I'm capable. I think I can do it."

"Nysa, I'm sorry. I have to say no. Sometimes we don't know what we really need, even for ourselves..."

"Mister Wolehead." Her voice, steady now. "Please."

Their eyes lock.
A pause.
A long moment.
He sighs.

"...Fine. What can I say? We'll try it, Nysa. But...at the first sign of fatigue, you come to me. We stop immediately. Promise me."

"I promise!"

Her face lights up. "Thank you, Mister Wolehead!"

Grinning widely, she exits the office. Her lungs pull in air—deep, full. Her hands rest against her chest, and she turns to face the hallway from the elevator.

"Finally coming home," she thinks, breathless with gratitude.
 "Ohh, so good to be back."

She steps in, presses four, takes three sips from her bottle—
 —when the elevator jolts to a stop.
 Two students' arms hold the doors open.

"Professor! Are you back? Are you well?"
 "How fantastic!"

She smiles quietly.

"Sorry to interrupt...we saw you from our class and ran after you..."
 "...to get your help with a step, Professor..."
 "...Yes, we've been struggling with..."

Amused, she lifts a hand.

"Yes, I'll help you. I was heading to my studio...it should be empty now. Come in. You'll show me the dance upstairs."

"Alright, do you have your song? Put it in the player, I'm watching...Just give me a second—I'll sit here.
I'm watching."

On the upbeat rhythm of Ray Charles' *Hallelujah, I Love Her So,* the duo launches into a swingy triple step, hips stretched, faces glowing with joy.

Nysa watches in silence, smiling.

"So, Professor—what do you think? We can't get the aerial after the twist swing-out. We keep missing the beat."

"Your weight isn't distributed correctly," she replies. "You're out of balance. Try again—don't open your legs so wide. You should feel the difference."

They nod, breathless, and turn to each other again.

Back into the routine—this time, tighter, more in sync.

"You see? So much better! You're hitting the beat now. Keep practicing—you'll get the lift right."

"Thank you so much, Professor!"
"If we pass, it'll be thanks to you! We missed you!"
"We all missed you. So excited you're back!"

Grinning, they hug, wave goodbye, and exit the studio.

A warmth rises in her chest as she turns toward the blackboard.
She hadn't seen it before.

WELCOME BACK, PROFESSOR! 

She smiles.
"Happy to be back, too," she murmurs.

Rolling the master chair behind the desk, she pauses before exiting the room. At the glass door, she catches her reflection.

Her fingertips brush the fabric of her pants.
Still watching herself, she slips her hand into her pocket.

The dice.
Warm. Soothing.

Slowly, she pulls it out, opens her palm.

"Even number—I made the right decision.
Odd... I'm skipping steps..."

She sighs.
Breathes in deep.
And tosses the die into the air.
Catches it. Closes her hand.

A long exhale.

Her gaze shifts to the studio behind her. She lowers her hand... slides it back into her pocket.

She stares at her reflection in the glass.

"I guess it's 'Until tomorrow,' then..."

V.

"What stands when all is seen?"

23.

She presses the elevator button. The doors slide open.

"Oh! Good evening, Professor. Are you back?"
Marq steps aside, making room for her.

"Good evening, Marq. I guess I am."
"Ground floor?"
"Yes, please. Thank you, Marq."
"Oh no, don't mention it... of course."

A knot tightens in her stomach. Her pulse jumps at her neck.
She inhales—quietly.
Is he staring at me?

She turns her head slowly.

He is. A polite smile plays on his lips, still staring.

"Marq... is there something on my face?"
"Oh...no. Sorry, Professor," he answers quickly, still smiling. He turns back toward the doors.
"Ground floor. You have arrived. Take care, Professor."

She hesitates.
"You're not getting out? Not going home?"

"Not yet," he says, still smiling. "I should be able to go very soon, I believe."

157

Something in her gut coils tighter.
She squints. Her brain stutters.
Her feet pivot. Her mouth opens without permission:

"...I'll go with you."

He nods, wordless, and reaches for her arm.

The doors close again. This time: to the basement.

The Core.
Her breath halts. Her body stiffens.
Why is he coming here again? And at this hour?

They walk.
The corridor darkens with each step. The air thickens.

"Marq... do you really need something in the archives now? It's late. I can help you tomorrow if—"

She stops.
He turns.

Her body locks.

"It is quite late indeed... *Nysa.*
To find the truth.
You shall not leave without it."

Nysa?
Since when does he call me by my first—?

The ground hums.
Her skin prickles.
Something behind her eyes goes dark.

The Core.
There it is. Ahead. Silent. Closed. Watching.

The tremor beneath her feet deepens. A hum, almost a growl.
Her knees buckle.

"Marq... what's going on?"
But no sound escapes her lips.

His voice distorts—rattling the walls:
"Those who hide...
Masks... trapped...
...shall not leave without the truuuuuuuth."

Her head spins.
Her vision bleeds at the edges.
The world lurches.

She falls—limbs folding like a marionette—
To the cold, hard floor.

The cold of her hands—piercing—shakes her awake.
"Marq! What..." she gasps, spinning her head, searching.

He's there. Kneeling in front of her, palms pressed to hers.
But it's not the Marq she knew.
Something's... changed.

With effort and fury, she pushes him away.
He obeys. Steps back. Silent. Still.

The look in his eyes steals her breath.
Without a word, he raises his hands. Two streams of glittering snowflakes rise with them, swirling through the air, entwined like vines of frozen light.
They circle her. Waist. Ankles. Wrists.
She opens her mouth—to scream? to speak?
—but it freezes.

She pulls. Kicks. Fights the glittering hold—
And stops.

A sigh. A surrender.
She rises, still wrapped in the snow.
Takes a step forward. Another. A third.

With each footfall, the glitter fades, giving way to a darkened ground.
The light dims, until the only thing she sees is her shadow stretching long over jagged stone.

Her arms tingle. She looks down.
 The marks.

Heart racing, she slips her hand into her pocket.
 The paper—wrinkled, familiar.
 She unfolds it.

There. The child.
 Frail. Sickly. Yellow eyes staring through time.

She stares back. Minutes pass. Maybe hours. Maybe lifetimes.

She breathes in. Exhales deeper.
 Nods. Bites her lip. Looks up.

"Okay. If this is what it takes.
 You and me. Now."

The ground trembles. Her vision blurs.
 And the child appears—flesh and bone. Frail. Bare ribs. Hollowed face.

"Finally," he says. "You're here."
 "Yes," she replies. "Let's get this over with."

In one sharp flick of his wrist, he hurls a stream of dark, glittering ice—shards that slash at her neck.

She arches, rising on the tips of her toes, eyes shut tight.
 And in one long, quiet inhale, lets herself fall back to her
heels.

The shards hit. Slice.
 She drops.

Her palms slam the ground. Bleeding.
 She rises again.

He grins.
 Black teeth. Poison.

He squeezes the air.
 More shards.

She drops.
 Rises.

Again.

More.

Rip—skin, bone, breath.
 She drops.
 Rises.

Her voice trembles in her mind:
 "How can I keep going?"
 She falls.
 Stands again.

"I don't know how to make it."
Falls.
Up. Again.

You took my blood. My hair. My flesh.
 "What more can you—argh!"
She crumples.
 Climbs back up.

"I just can't quit. Not now."

Falls.
 Rises.

"I cannot continue..."

Falls.
 Rises.

And then—
 A laugh. Far off. Twisted. Echoing through the blood and
fog.

She stumbles. Her body failing.
 Shards embedded deep. Blood pooling.
 Her lungs strain for air.
 She falls—slow, silent.

Eyes closing.

"I can't win. I can't stop..."

A voice.

"You don't have to. You did."

Her eyes snap open.
 Her ears ring with silence.

A stream of glittering snow snakes through the air—
 Wrapping the child's throat.

The laugh fades.
 The silhouette disintegrates.

Gone.

And where the door once stood, a message glows:

What truth is calling now?

She turns—spinning—mouth open, words trapped.

Marq?

Then, in a flash—
 Darkness.

Her thoughts, empty.
 Her body sinks.

Deeper.
 Deeper.
 Into numbness.

SHALL NOT LEAVE
WITHOUT THE TRUTH

24.

The next day
5:40 AM – 610 Greenhole Square

She wakes in her bed, with a dry mouth and aching limbs.

The room is quiet. Still. Dim light leaks in through the blinds, casting thin, silver lines across the ceiling. Her eyes trace them, hoping they might lead to clarity, to something she forgot—but the space in her mind is blank.

No pain. No dream. No sound.
Just the hollow throb of something missing.

She blinks.

The ceiling doesn't answer.

Her body feels unfamiliar in its stillness, as if it had weathered a storm without her. She places one hand on her chest, steady—too steady—and breathes in. A stale, shallow breath. It doesn't reach her ribs.

She swings her legs to the edge of the bed and lets them drop. Her bare feet touch the cold floor. She follows, sliding down the mattress until she's on the ground.

Eyes wide open.

And she stays there.

Not searching.
 Not crying.
 Not remembering.

Just being.

For some time.

Eyes blank, jaw slack, her finger drifts slowly across the ridges of the marks.
 Tingling.

A jolt of pain stings her, and she gasps.
 "Oh no... Thorne," she whispers, pressing her palm hard against her forearm, as if trying to contain the pain. Her lips curl inward. "Does he feel this, too?"

Her breath shortens. She winces, brows furrowing deeply.
 "I need to speak with Thorne."

Dazed, she rises from the floor like smoke off embers—slowly, blindly. Her gaze falls on the mirror above her dressing table.

She stares.

At the shape of her hair. Frayed, untamed. Foreign.
 "What happened with my hair? Why is it shorter?" she mutters, the question floating in the room unanswered. Her eyes remain locked. Her mind, still a few steps behind.

Her hand moves toward the table. Fingers find the scissors. Cold metal in a trembling grip.
 Snip.
 A section falls.
 She exhales.
 Deep breath in.

Snip.
 Pause.

Snip.

More hair falls to the floor in soft, weightless curls.

One last look at her reflection.
 "...Different," she murmurs. Not a judgment. Not quite acceptance.
 Just... an observation.

She reaches for the small, transparent bottle by her nightstand.
 Three sips. A sharp breath through her nose.

And then—without hesitation—
 Heads to The Center.

In room 4-202, sitting cross-legged on the floor, she sees him.

Thorne.

Quietly, on the balls of her feet, she steps in. Her movements—soft, careful—as if worried she might disrupt the stillness he brings.
"Nysa, what are you doing? This is your room," she scolds herself, but keeps walking.

She settles beside him. Close, but not too close.

Timidly, she glances his way. His chin looks sharper, she thinks. Did he lose weight again?

He looks up. A faint, gentle smile flickers on his lips. He lowers his gaze back to his hands.

"Long time no see," she murmurs. "You disappeared. I haven't seen you since..."
She hesitates.
"Since our... dance."

Her pulse quickens. He says nothing.

She clears her throat. Looks down. Tries again.

"I felt something this morning," she says, brushing her fingertips across the marks on her forearm. "Pain."

He watches her silently, the corner of his mouth lifting in a brief smile. It fades just as quickly.

"I thought of you and came to check if..."
She shakes her head. A deep inhale.
"Never mind."

Then, quieter:
"I was thinking... I never really asked about you. Where have you been all these years? Where did you live? What your life looked like... before."

"What do you want to know?" he asks, voice even.

Her heart beats faster. She clenches her fist slightly.

"I... I'm not sure."

He studies her for a moment. Nods.

"Alright. Let me go first. What brought you here? To teach?"

She straightens her posture, surprised by the question. "My passion."

He raises an eyebrow.

"For music," she adds.

"And...?"

She shrugs lightly. "That's it. I love dance. Music. This place."

A pause.

"I see," he says. "Not very talkative today?"

"No—yes. I talk. I know you saved me. With the shard. The other day."
Her fingers nervously toy with the hem of her skirt.

He looks at her again. Then simply nods.

Lowering his eyes back to his hands, to the forearms marked like hers, he clears his throat and asks:

"What's your favorite food?"

She arches a brow, amused. "Salmon. Why?"

He pulls a face. "Ugh. I hate salmon."

She laughs. And just like that, the air between them shifts.

"What's your favorite place?" he asks.

"Here in the city? Easy," she replies. "The Center. Outside of it? Anywhere warm, green, quiet. A park, with trees that creak a little when the wind passes through."

She pauses, leans in a little—just enough to bridge the breath of space between them.
 "What about you?"

He shrugs, his voice low. "I enjoy traveling. But if I had to choose... I'd say home."

She tilts her head, amused. "Mysterious answer. Home—where is that for you?"

Silence.

She watches him for a moment. Exhales through her nose and lets it go.

"Okay. Never mind... Your favorite number?"

"Six."

"Favorite song?"

"Too many."

"Color?"

"White."

"Mine's yellow," she grins. "Book?"

"..."

"..."

"..."

She laughs. "Okay, okay, tough crowd. Fine. Let's try this: most hated quote?"

"That's easy," he says, "'what doesn't kill you—'"

"—makes you stronger!" she finishes with mock horror. "Ugh. I *hate* that one too! I even made up a worse version, I repeat to myself when I'm in a really dramatic mood."

They both break into laughter—sharp, open, unexpected.

"Wow," she says, catching her breath. "That was... not where I thought this was going."

"Unexpectedly fun?" he lifts a brow.

She nods. "Exactly that."

A beat. Her expression softens.

"You know... I think I might've been wrong about you. Maybe I owe you an apology."

"*Might*?" he smirks.

"Okay, fine!" she laughs. "For misjudging you. It's not a huge deal, but..."

"Oh, not a big deal, huh?" he grins, nudging her shoulder lightly.

She chuckles, straightens a little, and looks at him sincerely. "I apologize."

He nods, slowly. "Apology accepted."

Then, with a grin: "You know, this is kinda nice—but let's not forget I could still wipe the floor with you if we battled."

She scoffs, flicking his arm. "Please. I'd destroy you."

Their laughter lingers, but fades with her next inhale. Her smile falters.

"Your marks, Thorne."

He meets her eyes. "Hmm?"

"Where did you get them?"

She starts to raise her hand toward his forearm, as if drawn to the familiar pattern etched in his skin, but stops herself, retreating.

He notices. Frowns faintly. "I'm not sure. I've had them as long as I can remember. They just... showed up. Grew with me."

She listens closely as he tells her about their first appearance, how they darkened with time, how they became less strange and more like a second skin.

Curious again, she lifts her hand—then pulls it back.

"Your wife," she blurts, catches herself. "Or... ex-wife. Did she have them too?"

He lets out a short laugh.

"I didn't take you for someone who listens to rumors. Maybe I misjudged you, too."

"I don't. I heard... that. And about your temper."

His smile dims. He turns his eyes to the floor.

"Some say I can't control my anger."

A quiet smile plays on her lips. Images rise in her memory...
...a girl on the floor, fists pounding the ground...
...a soft toy flung across the room...
...metal torn from something once whole...
...a scream swallowed in silence.

She murmurs, "Yeah. I can relate."

His shoulders ease. His eyes lift.

"Some even say I can summon thunder."

She squints at him playfully. "That would explain all the lightning in your photos."

He chuckles. It's soft. Warm.

She straightens, curious. "Thorne... where did you learn to dance?"

He lifts his chin toward the window. "In the streets. From the rain—shapeless, unpredictable."

She lifts a brow. He continues:

"From the storms. From the wind. Fast. Unapologetic."

She chuckles. "Starting to understand those psychiatric rumors now."

He doesn't laugh. But he doesn't shrink either.

"My parents. They were home. But never really *there*.
I liked going out. The noise of the outside. The storms.
The thunder made the silence less... oppressive.
And, honestly speaking? They give quite a good beat."

They both remain quiet. Head looking down, wordless.

"I just grew to like them. The cold. The night. The noise."

"And danger?" she adds.

He doesn't reply.
She doesn't push.
The silence sits between them, unspoken, understood.

She's easier to talk to now.
She listens.
Not like before—
When she let you down.

He's actually... trustworthy.
He understands more
than I thought.

Her lips part again.
"Is it true? Were you expelled? Not allowed to come back?"

He meets her gaze. Steady. Quiet.
"I became invisible to the world.
But how long can one be defined by others' perception?"
A pause. "I knew this place would always take me back."

He draws a slow breath.
"I came back for a reason. With a goal.
And it's vital that I achieve it."

He says no more.
She thinks to respond, then lets the moment pass.

They sit together, still and silent.

In his mind, fragments swirl—
...a boy, alone in the storm...
...spinning barefoot on a rain-slick street...
...ruins echoing with thunder...
...each movement syncing with the sky.

In hers, warmth blooms—
...a dinner table, crowded and loud...
...cheaters in board games getting called out...
...siblings laughing until they cried...
...Saturdays filled with joy and noise.

Fingers find fingers.
 And quietly, they intertwine.
  Hearts beating steadily, synchronized by the quiet knowing
 of what it is to feel...
Like the odd one.

25.

Moments later, her head dips. Fatigue begins to settle in.

She glances over at him and smiles.
"Hey. Are you tired too?"

"No." He smiles back. "Are you?"

"Yes. I need to go home. Rest. Change for my evening class."

"Okay."

She shifts her knees and moves to rise—
 But something catches.

She looks down—her fingers are still threaded in his.

She clears her throat and laughs softly.
 Unlaces her hand.

"Thank you, Thorne. For the... quiet. That was really nice."

"Yes, Nysa. I'll see you later."

She walks out slowly. No rush.
 Shoulders lowering.
 Chest fuller.
 Breath easier.

"How unexpected," she thinks, the words melting into a smile.

Her steps quicken as she reaches the main floor.
Destination: Maisha's place.
"So much to tell her!"

Out on the street, a soft breeze brushes her cheek. A thought touches her mind—gentle, sudden.

She slides her hobo bag onto one shoulder, unzips the front pocket.

Her sketchbook is already open—
'Grandpa holding his watch.'

She smiles, brushing her fingers across the pencil marks on his face.

A quiet breath.

She turns the page. Blank. Waiting. Pulls out her 2B pencil.

And begins to draw. Without hesitation.

As if she already knows what image needs to live there next:

To her right, fifty meters from the billboard, she spots the wooden staircase on RedBricks Avenue.

Climbing to the second floor, she catches her breath as she pushes open the heavy wooden door.

She pulls her jacket tighter over her shoulders and steps into the apartment.

Inside, she slips off her shoes and places them on the rough, U-shaped tree trunk cabinet—its leatherwood scent rising to meet her.

As she moves down the corridor, her nose twitches. Spicy wood. Warm vanilla. The familiar comfort lingered in the air.

She hears it before she sees it.

Leaning silently on the doorframe of the beige-and-green furnished living room, she takes in the scene:

Maisha, waiting with a steaming teapot in one hand, tapping the cozy armchair beside her with the other.

"Taking off my jacket," Nysa murmurs.

Maisha smiles gently. Her silver rock pendant sways softly against her chest.

"Sit. Drink your rooibos. It's still warm."

Nysa settles in, her body sinking into the velvety fabric of the chair.

"Maisha," she says, eyes lowered, voice tight. "There are things I need to tell you.
 Questions I need to ask. Things have been happening... things I don't understand."

Maisha pours the tea in silence, her lean fingers graceful in their movement. She glances up, quietly.

"What's been in your mind, child? And in your drawings?"

Nysa blinks. "In my drawings?"

The older woman takes a slow sip. Her gaze remains steady.

"Paths sometimes appear... only when we are ready to see them."

She rises without another word and gestures subtly toward the hallway.

"You can sleep here tonight. After your class. Or now, if you'd like. Don't worry about the tea—I'll take care of it."

Nysa nods faintly, her hands wrapped around the cooling cup.

She finishes the last sip, stands, and glances once more at the empty chair.

From her bag, she pulls out a small pouch of candies and places it on the table.

A soft breeze brushes the back of her neck. She shivers, exhales.

Grabbing her jacket from the hanger, she walks down the corridor toward the guest room.
 Her head feels heavy. Her mind, fogged.

Still so many questions... and even fewer answers.

She lays her head on the pillow, the cotton ear curled gently in her palm, and turns off the light.

This time... I'll get my answers, she hears herself think.

And falls back into *the* dream.

26.

The long, dark corridor.
 Sewage-scented.
 Humid.
 Lanterns hang along the walls, flickering with uneven light.

Dozens of steps forward—her shoulders graze the walls, skin scratched raw.

The sparkle again.
 The Child in the mirror.
 His voice cuts through the thick silence:

"How could you forget?"

She breathes in sharply: "You tried to kill me."

The Child says nothing.

She steadies her voice: "How could I forget *what*?"

No answer.

"Forget what?", she repeats.

Still silence.

"Tell me. You can trust me."

Nothing.

"Please. How could I forget what?"

A pause.

"Forget…"
The Child's voice wavers.
"…that I'm scared of the shadows."

A beat.

"I told you already.
I always tell you."

Her breath catches in her throat. Her chest tightens. Her jaw clenches—and then loosens.

"I remember now," she says, voice low.
Eyes locked onto his, she inhales. Holds it.
Exhales.
Inhales again.

The Child. The corridor. The dimming lanterns.

She smiles gently, tilting her chin toward the lights.
"Do they always go out like this?"

The Child nods. "Always."

She steps closer to the mirror.

"You won't need those lanterns again.
I promise."

The flames flicker again, shrinking.

Inside the mirror, the Child watches her. Unblinking. Intense.

Suddenly, warmth flares in her chest. She feels it radiating outward.

From inside?
 Is that... me?

The warmth grows. The light glows. Expands.

Is that me... doing that?

Her voice echoes inside her skull, awed and uncertain.
 Light pours from her chest. Fills the corridor.
 Bathes the walls. Splashes the mirror.

Something falls behind her with a soft clink.
 The lanterns blink out.

Darkness—except for her.
 Glowing.

She doesn't flinch. She doesn't hide.

The Child watches.
 And slowly... smiles.

They step forward.
 Out of the mirror.

"I have something for you," they say softly.

She swallows, blinking through the light.
 "Something for me?"

The Child opens their hand, palm facing up
— Nysa freezes.

Torn, as old as time,
A stuffed, greyish, smelly
Ear-shaped cotton piece.

Hand covering her mouth, she holds her breath.
Her fingers carefully extend and brush the cotton piece.
"The other ear…" she says in a whisper
"I thought I had lost it."

Her fingers brush the ripped ear. Hold it. Grab it gently.
Squeeze it.

With a smile, she exhales and lets her lungs fill in. Her
eyes open wide.
Look at the child again.

Watch them wave at her. Breathe. Smile. And vanish.

A soft ping stirs in her stomach.
 She walks to the mirror.

Nothing.
 No reflection.
 No Child.

She leans in. Brow furrowed. Waits.

Then—
 There.

The Child appears again. Waving. Smiling.
 Looking fuller now. Stronger. Whole.

"You've got a new shirt," she laughs gently, eyes
misting. "And not ripped this time. Fantastic."

The cotton ear still pressed in her palm, she tilts her
chin up, steady now.

"You were always a *she*," she whispers.
 A pause.
 "You were always *me*."

The Child doesn't reply. Just smiles one last time—softly, knowingly.
 And fades.

Swallowed by a blooming pool of white light.

The mirror empties.

And in its place, six words form, etched in radiant clarity:

What...
 stands when...
 all...
 is...
 seen?

VI.

"What rises when survival ends?"

27.

I feel... warm.

 At peace.

 Full.

 Like I've eaten and drunk a feast meant for someone finally welcomed home.

I dress for my final class of the evening and pass by Maisha's room.

 "Maisha, I'll return to my apartment tonight. Thank you again."

 "Always, dear. I'll see you soon."

Later. After class.
11:46 PM — 610 Greenhole Square

I step into my home.

Still glowing.

The warmth in my chest hasn't faded.
 If anything—it's grown.
 The walls look brighter. The furniture is softer. Even the
air... it smells like a memory. Maybe joy.
 Even my brand-new mattress somehow looks warmer. As
if it waited for me to believe I deserved it.

I place a palm to my chest—where the light rose in the
dream.
 Close my eyes.
 Let the silence wrap around me like soft cotton.
 And breathe.

My hand reaches into my purse. I pull out the ear.
 Cotton. Whole. Solid.
 Not just a dream.

I place it beside its twin.
 And smile.

I glance toward the lamp, ready to switch off the light—
 But something pulls me back.
 A small mountain of unused pillows next to the bed.

Suddenly, my mind drifts—
 Family.
 Laughter.
 Shouting over board games.
 Saturday night talent shows.
 Togetherness.

And then, as if called forward—
 Grief.
 Loss.
 Messy relationships.
 Aching love.
 The slow, quiet unraveling of what I thought was
"home."

Therapy words echo: *abandonment issues, avoidant tendencies, solitude as self-protection...*
 "Buzzwords a therapist would love," I whisper with a half-smirk.

But I stare at the pillows—and for the first time...
 They feel unnecessary.
 Misplaced.
 As if they were guarding something I no longer need hidden.

I raise my arm.
 Gently push them to the edge.
 And let them fall.
 Soft thuds on the floor.

On my bedside, the sketch I drew earlier catches my eye.
 My heart skips.
 Maisha's voice, still echoing—
 "What's been in your drawings lately?"

I breathe in.
 Pull the heavy blanket over me.
 Sink into the mattress.
 Lighter now.
 Though still... heavy.

I feel—
 like it's been
 a lot.

I am exhausted.

I open my eyes.
Look around.
"Where am I?"
Oh... right. My apartment.

Memories from last night—
and the night before that,
and the days before that—
stir back to life in my mind.

Something tightens in my chest.
I reach for my phone.
Check the date.

And there it is—
The knot.

"Oh no.
It's *that* time of the month.
Again."

28 a.

I drop the phone.
 Drag the heavy blanket over my head.
 Shut the world out.
 Eyes closed.

Heartless—
 quite literally—
 the alarm screams again.

With a sigh soaked in dread,
 I roll to my right.
 Hit it.
 Hard.
 Throw it across the room.

Eyes puffy.
 Body heavy.
 I get up.
 Get dressed.
 Get out.

And go.

Moments later
At The Ancient Place

And here I am again.
 Regular as clockwork.

Same smell.
 Same colors.
 Same cold.

I slip off my jacket and walk straight to the wall.
 The tiny dots of blood from last time are gone—
 the surface is perfectly clean,
 as if they never existed.

I roll up my sleeves.
 Press both forearms flat against the muddy stone.
 A tear wells in the corner of my eye.
 I wipe it away with my finger.

Then I lower myself down—
 onto the floor,
 on my back,
 face and palms turned skyward.

The temperature drops.
 And I feel it again.

The shard.
The glass.
The sickle.

It scrapes beneath my veins.

I clench both fists—
 and stop moving.

The frost stabs my lungs.
 The hammer strikes my bones.

Soon, my veins begin to tear.
 And my mind starts to numb.

That's when I begin to feel less—
 less of the clots,
 the cracks,
 the crumbles.
Less of the world.

My spirit rises above my body.
 To escape.

Far in the distance, voices echo—
 "The Marked Ones... said to hold great power...
 scars so visible... success in battle..."

My lungs hold my breath.
 My brain drowns in clouds.

Still, the voices speak.
And then—
an image.

A light.
A silhouette.

"I know it can be cold. Can it not?"
A warm, gravelly voice.

"Who are you?" I ask.

A sway. Something swinging back and forth—
a pendant? A rock?

"Maisha?"

"I much prefer The Sun," he replies.

The light in front of me sharpens.

A tall, white-haired man stands there—
chubby, with a cane,
a heavy silver rock pendant hanging at his chest.

"Are you Maisha's dad?" I ask, my voice faint.

He doesn't answer. Just smiles.

I turn to look around—
no body.
No room.

No wall.
Just smoke.

White.
Grey.
And the man.

"I've always loved The Sun," he says.
 "It's light...so bright, so wide.
  It illuminates half the Earth at once. Isn't that something?"

"I like the Sun too," I whisper. "And the warmth. I don't like the cold."

"Many do," he says. "They seek The Sun's light to see. Its heat to feel. Its presence to feel safe...Isn't it a gift?"

He steps closer, light dancing across his face.

"An unwavering ally...strong, reliable...offering treasures every single day. Without fail. Never late. Never absent."

His voice fades a little,
 but the warmth in my chest grows.
 Calm.

Peace.

He studies me.
 Speaks again.

"How far does yours shine?"

I frown. Shake my head.
 He holds my gaze.

"Mine? What?"

"Your light," he says.
 "How far and wide does *your* light shine?"

My lips part.
 Teeth bite tongue.
 No sound.

I glance at my forearms.

"An outside ally is a blessing," he says, gently.
 "But an inside one, Nysa...an inner Sun...that's power."

I squint against the light.
 Open my mouth.

"Sir...Am I... a Marked One?"

I raise my eyes—
 but the smoke's already fading.

The space where he stood is now
 completely
 empty.

Air comes in again. I feel my cells breathing—
streams of oxygen rushing, surging through my veins.
The pain is still there, but fading.

I push up on my elbows and start my body scan:
Toes—*yes, they're working.*
Back of my feet—*still alive.*
Twist my ankles—*good, still moving.*
Rotate the knees—*check.*
Lower back—*okay.*
Upper chest—*still rising.*

...

One more day: I survived.

...

I exhale.

Wiping the dirt from my clothes, I walk toward the wall
again.
The tiny dots of blood now shimmer faintly.
I glance back at the ground where I had been lying... then
up—
To The Sun.
Bright. Wide.

I take a deep breath in and press both palms to the wall.
It's hot.
Humid.
Not cold like before.

My hands tremble. I pull away.
Eyes closed, I see it—
that light in my chest.
The one that feels peaceful. Warm.

I open my eyes again.
Squint.
Look at my hand.

The wind stirs. Stones tremble on the floor.
I hold my breath.
Squint harder.

The wind grows stronger.
The stones begin to roll.

My palm opens—
and a ray of light appears.
Long. Thin.

A shard.
A *glass* shard?

Did I just summon that?

Images rush in: pain, blood, cuts.
 The shard rises, sharp and dangerous—
 exactly like that night in The Center.
 It rotates.
 Then begins to fracture—
  thin golden veins spreading across it, dancing like
filaments of light.
 They weave together and merge.

The shard drops into my palm.
 Sharp. Cold.
 But beautiful—
 glass braided with gold.

I kneel by the wall.
 Brush its surface.

My hand finds a crack.
 I close my eyes.
 Feel the light inside my chest once more.

When I open them, the shard rises again,
 drawn to the crack like a compass to true north.

I guide it forward.
 It slips in.
 Deeper.
 And deeper.

The golden veins,
 seeping into the wall.

And I whisper to the once-dreaded wall:
"It's yours now."

The wind howls.

Golden light spreads across the wall,
 veins expanding, glowing.
 Smoke curls from the cracks.
 Something clinks to the ground.

I look down—
 A pendant.
 A silver rock pendant.

I blink.
 Rub my eyes.

Maisha's pendant?

I pick it up.
"Do you mind?" I whisper, not knowing who I'm asking.

The wind answers, brushing past me.
 I squint again—
 The pendant fractures, golden veins threading through
the silver.

I slip it over my neck.
 The wall trembles again.

Silence.

I breathe in,
 and a single tear rolls down my cheek—
 yellow and bright, like golden light.

I wipe it away with my sleeve,
 watch it fall gently into one of my marks.
 And just like that—
 It vanishes.

I lift my eyes to the wall.
 Around the shard, the tiny dots are now connected by
thin, red lines.

Words:

What if one was never broken?

Air floods my lungs.
 I breathe deeply.

A thought flickers in my mind—
 What does not break you...
 But this time, I stop it.

I don't want the pressure.
 The expectation.

The need to prove anything.
To please.
To be understood.

I just want lightness.
Silence.
And space
to breathe.

I turn.
Walk out.
The wind pushes gently against my face.

And I know—
We *both* know—
I'll be back.

Regular as clockwork.

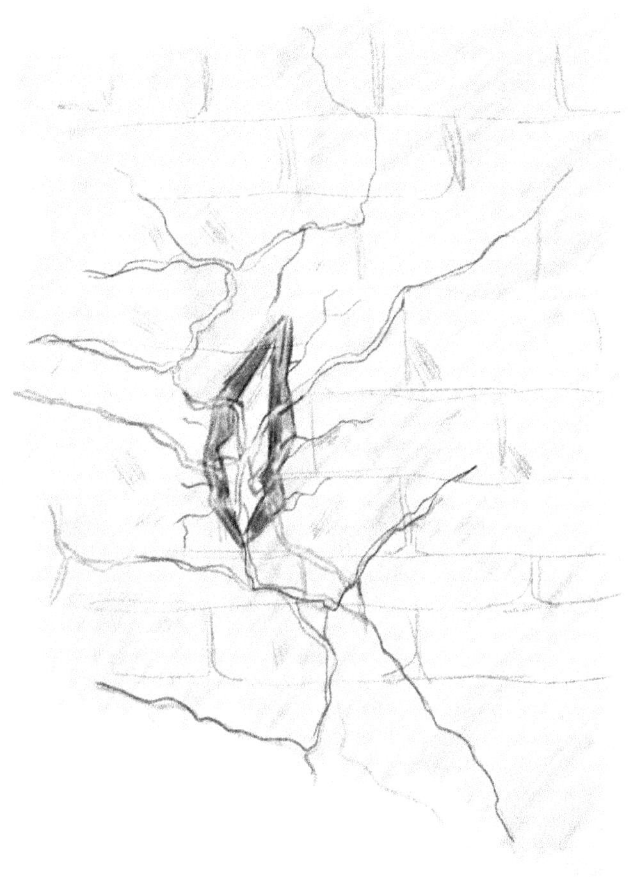

28 b.

Moments later
In the same Greek battle arena
— Maisha speaking

I felt his presence. In my chest.
 And I ran.

"It is so good to see you."
 — Silence.
 Just like I knew he would.
 That's what he always does when he's mad.

"Dad." He looks at me.
 Again, like I knew he would.

"Will you cut my wings?"

He smiles—tilts his head slightly, eyes meeting mine.

"You've always given everything to your family. To protect
your loved ones. I know that's what she is to you."

He pauses.

"You've always shown wisdom, Maisha. You protect."

His eyebrow lifts. The smile fades from his lips.

"But you also know this...when it comes to helping others...There are rules. There's a speed to healing when you use your power. But in powerlessness...you give the other..."

"...the gift of discovery," I finish softly.

He nods.
I smile and lift my eyes to the sky with him.

"I remember, Dad. I've heard you say it before...I just always had my doubts about that theory..."

I feel his hand rest gently on my shoulder.
Warm. Grounding.
And before I can say another word—
He vanishes into smoke.

I close my eyes.

"But I'm learning it now. Thank you, Dad," I whisper.

In my mind, the vision of Nysa—
lying breathless, at the mercy of her own demons—
resurfaces.

How certain can I be,
I ask silently,
that she's ready to make these decisions on her own?
That it's time for me to step out?

I breathe in,
trusting—
knowing—
he can hear me still.

And I walk away.

29.

I stare at my sketches, mind blank.

Three elements.
Three disruptions that shattered my sense of control.
And yet... somehow, I feel calm.
Almost... *ok*.

I try to analyze, to make sense of what I've drawn—
But no clear meaning emerges.
It's as if the whole world has gone quiet.

I know I feel things...
but I can't tell you what.
I know I can see things...
but I'm not sure which.

Pencil between my teeth, spinning slowly around my fingers,
 I sigh. Long and low.

I rise from my chair, set the pencil down, grab my jacket—
 and step outside.

The hot rays strike my skin,
 and the warmth, at once, presses against my body—
awakens something.

My mind spins.
 The words return, clear as glass:
 "An outside ally is such a great power. An inside one, Nysa…"

The old man's voice—
 still lingering somewhere in my bones.

I tilt my head back.
 The star above, yellow and magnetic, pulses like a memory.
 In a silent plea for comfort, I close my eyes.
 And then—
 I open them again.

"What if…"

My gaze lands on the rooftop of The Center.
Suddenly, I'm running.

By the time I reach the top,
 The Sun blinds me. I squint, breathless.
 My jacket slips off my shoulders.
 I let it fall.

My arms—bare.
 My marks—burning.
 Glowing under the skin.

They are calling.

I lift my head again, and darkness meets me.
 Grey clouds swallow The Sun.
 Its shield of comfort—gone.
 So quickly, it hurts.

Still, I keep my chin high.
 And stare.

The sky unravels in chaos.
 Thunder. Storm.
 Bolts crackle through clouds like broken bones.
 Rain lashes the rooftop, ice-cold, slicing through the air.
 My muscles seize, skin tightens.
 My eyes burn.

But I don't look away.
 I *feel* it all.

I inhale deeply.
 And exhale—steadily.

The thunder claps again. Louder.
And I feel its rhythm in my chest.
A beat. A calling.

I throw my hands up.
And from the sky, two streams of rain rise—
twisting upward in spirals, like serpents made of water.
S-shaped, gleaming, climbing above the clouds.

I raise my arms higher,
 pulse pounding.

I kick the ground—
 hard.

The water streams collide,
 burst—
  and fall into a downpour of brilliant, razor-sharp
droplets.

Splash.

I scream.
 It's freezing.
 It's *powerful*.

I drop to my knees,
 laughing, gasping—alive.

"I don't need to look outward for warmth.
Or power.

I don't need The Sun.
It's all within me."

And then—
from the air around me, they rise.

Two streams of glimmering snowflakes.
Intertwined.
Dancing.

They circle me gently—
a silent crown.

Before my feet, a golden path unfurls—
lined with shimmering snowflakes, glowing like constellations.

Words begin to form.
Letters drift together:

What can one see now?

I smile.
Because now, I *can* see.
And at the end of that golden path, rising into the sky—
I know what's waiting.

30.

Hours later
9:48 PM – The Center's Performance Theater

This is it.
 This is the moment.

I need to dance.

Not to shine.
 Not to be perfect.
 Not to impress.

Just to be—
 authentic.
 Free.
 And happy.

And somehow, I know... he feels it too.

Once a year, The Center opens its doors.
 Dancers, students, professors, and lovers of the craft—
 All are welcome to share their art with the world.

I had prepared all year for a solo performance.
 But not tonight.
 Tonight, I need to dance with him.

I race to the fourth floor—Studio 4-202.
 And there he is.

Stretching in front of the blackboard.
 Like he always belonged there.

"Thorne!"
I bend over, catching my breath.
 "I'm so glad you're here."

"I figured you might need a strong partner," he says with a smile. "I came to warm up."

"Listen—there's a freestyle category. I'll register your name and—"

"Relax," he interrupts, calm.
 "You follow my lead."

"10:33 PM. Seven minutes," I whisper.
"They'll call us in seven."

"I'm ready, Nysa."
His voice is steady.
"Because I trust *you*. You're sharp. You're grounded.
You're real.
Breathe. We'll be fine."

"Okay."
But my breath is already gone.

"Nysa? Thorne?
You're up in two!"

"Now," he says gently.
"Just breathe.
And follow my lead."

Moments later
On Stage

The stage is dark.

She enters first, back turned to the audience.
 Shadow outlined by the faint glow behind her.

She breathes in—
 And holds.

The first note rings out.

Thorne enters from the right.
 A single spotlight crowns him.

She spins left—
 He strikes thunder with his feet on the right.

Two separate rhythms.
 Two distinct worlds.

She chassés forward—sharp, fluid.
 He steps back, giving space, safety.

They move—
 She spirals.
 He waits.

Their eyes meet.

He bends, offers his hand.
 She spins around him.
 Doesn't take it.

His lips move silently: *"It won't break from a firm grip."*

She laughs—
 a spiral again—
 then bends...
 and takes his hand.
 Gently.

The lights dim—
 then flare, bright.

She releases.
 Then grabs again.

"Catching, not *shaking your hand now,"* she whispers.

He smiles. Pulls her closer.
 Their breath synchronizes, rising fast.

Under her sleeve, the marks glow.
 His too.
 He feels the burn—
 The fire.

She stares.
 Drops his hand.
 Pushes him away.

He folds again—
 pulls her back in.

A forward step.
 A push.
 Plié.
 Lift—drop.

Every movement...
 a word unsaid.
 A memory exhaled.
 A question, answered.

She pauses, off-beat.
 He waits.

She smiles.
 Starts to run.

He stops her—
 with a look.

They laugh.

Their fingers interlace.
 Her heel drops.
 She rises again.

They lower—
 foreheads close.

Lips closer.
Breath held.

The music stops.
The audience rises.

Silence.

He holds still.
Chin lifted.
Arms firm.

Outside—
lightning splits the sky.

She places her fingers on his cheek.
He exhales.

She inhales.
They exhale.

The final piano note drifts,
 and the chandelier scatters its light across their skin like
stars.

He guides her into the final fall.
She lands.
Spins.
Bends.

And runs into his arms.

The curtains fall.
Thunder and applause rise in unison.

But they hear only one thing—
The other's heartbeat.

Connected.
Fierce.
Authentic.
Calling.

Moments later
In room 4-202

We burst into the room—exhilarated, breathless, electrified by the fire we left on stage.
 Hot, wet, and shivering, we slide to the floor, laughter chasing silence.
 I lay my head against his chest, its rhythm still fast, still wild.

And we just... stay.
 Letting time melt into the night.

My heart fills—
 With heat.
 With life.
 With gratitude.

A smile lingers on my lips.
 My fingers trace the marks on his arms.
 And we remain quiet, suspended in the rare stillness of a moment that both of us know will flicker—
 Soon.

I open my hand, extend it to him.
 He hesitates.
 Then takes it.

"I like dancing with you," I say in a quiet voice.
 The words float gently into the space between us.

"You're not that arrogant after all," he replies. "I like dancing with you, too."

Our hearts—beating in wild sync—slowly begin to settle.
 He strokes my fingers with his thumb... releases.

"I cannot be with you."

It slices through me like a shard.

"Because you're too lonely...?" I whisper, barely audible.

He looks into my eyes—
 and breaks me again.

"I cannot be with you."

I breathe.
 Deep.
 Hold the silence.
 Savor it before it all unravels.

"So," he says, with a stillness that carries weight, "how do you feel?"

"I feel fear," I say.
 Pause.
 "Also peace."

Silence again.

I shift my legs to sit.
 He pulls me close.

"Come here," he says gently.

I lower myself again.

He stands.
 "Come over here."

I follow.
 He wraps his arms around my waist.

His jaw tenses slightly as I draw closer.
 He shakes his head, faintly. Smiles.

"What are you laughing at, you... Jerk!"
 We both laugh.

And again—quiet.
 I wait.
 Then ask:

"Is it because of your wife? Or... ex-wife? Or... someone?"

He raises an eyebrow.
 "You really like those gossip mill stories, don't you?"

I try to smile.
 It doesn't quite reach.

He lifts my chin.

"It's not because of my ex-wife."

"I understand," I say aloud.
 But inside, a softer voice replies: I don't...

He studies me.
 Then asks, again:
 "And now, how do you feel?"

I pause.

"I don't know... quiet.
 Like the silence before a storm."

He nods, slowly.
 Smiles.
 Gently grabs my arms, straightens them, and examines them.

"You might be ready now," he says softly.
 "Here—what do you see?"

I glance down.
 "My forearms. My scars..."

He smiles. Nods. Silent again.

Then—
 He takes my face between his palms.
 Kisses my eyelids.

"And here... what do you see?"

I laugh.
 "Nothing! I mean... my eyes."

He smiles again. Nods again.
 Leads me to the mirror.

"And on this pretty face—what do you see?"

I tilt my head.
 "My eyes. My nose. My lips?"

He turns my head gently.
 Kisses my neck.

"And now? How do you feel?"

"I..."

My breath catches.
 Pulse races.
 My chest burns with heat.
 I grip his arms—my knees are unsteady.

He kisses me again.

"And now?" he whispers.

"I feel like I'm..."

I try to breathe.
 I try to speak.

"I feel like I'm..."

"...whole."

The word escapes like a truth I never meant to say out loud—
 but it hangs in the air, undeniable.

"Thorne," I murmur, "I feel like I'm..."

My skin tingles. Every inch of it.
 I turn my head toward him—
 and then—

Light.

Blinding. Warm. Full.

"...whole."

The room pulses.
  The light dims. Flares brighten again, illuminating everything.
 But something's different now.

My palm presses against my belly.
 Instinctively.
 Like I'm guarding something fragile and alive.

I step to the mirror.
 I stare.

And staring back—

A young, bright, chubby boy.
Yellow eyes. Round cheeks. A softness I recognize.
And yet—
not from memory.
From me.

And then I hear him.

"I cannot be with you, Nysa..."

His voice—gentle, resigned.
Like it's the only way to protect me.

Tears stream down my cheeks, slow and burning.
Not from pain. Not even from sadness.

But from knowing.

“...because I am you.”

243

My legs tremble. Then fail.
 I drop to the ground, breathless, eyes still locked on the mirror.
 Tears fall, freely now—
 not out of grief,
 but recognition.

Blood rushes to my temples. My mind swims with fragments:
 Our marks... the same.
 Our stories... inverse.
 He was always sick when I was well...
 And well, when I was sick.
 Always present,
 always watching.
 Each time, I stood on the edge of losing myself.

In the noise of this revelation, only one question echoes—

Were you ever meant to be broken?

I close my eyes. Kneel.
 The tingling in my arms—gone.
 The marks on my forearms—smaller now, faded almost.
 I don't dare look back at the mirror.

I rise.

And I walk out of the studio, quietly.
 Up. I need to go up.

To the rooftop.
To the place where the air is thinner but the sky is louder.

My entire world feels like it's shattering—
and yet, in the same breath, aligning.

The weight on my shoulders is heavy.
But for the first time...
There's no more weight in my stomach.

Tonight, I will summon storms.
Thunders.
Pain.
Anger.
Overwhelm.
Loss.

This shadow—this dark, jagged part of me I've always buried and blamed—
has to come out.

Now.

Or I may never find my way out of it.

31.

A few weeks later
1:12 PM – Destination: The Center, 41 Liapsar Boulevard

"Yes, Maisha, I'm on my way.
 Almost there! I'll meet you in the lobby!"

I end the call and weave through the city's noise, dodging impatient cars and sighing at every stubborn crosswalk.

Liapsar Boulevard...
 One more turn. Serves Street...
 270 meters... and I'm there.

With a confident smile and lightness in my chest, I lift my head toward the building.
 My second home for the last four years.
 A place where—undeniably—magic happens.

At the entrance, I catch my reflection in the laminated glass doors.
 Shoulders square. Deep breath in.
 Furtive smile.

I step inside.

Maisha is already waiting by the elevators. As the doors glide open, I glance at the sepia square where Thorne's photo used to hang.
"Did it fall for good this time?" I wonder.
But I don't ask.

We exit on the fourth floor and walk in silence down the corridor.
I've never cared much for "end of year" vibes—
But there's something comforting about today's stillness.

We reach Room 4-202 and sit in the chairs near the wide window.
Outside, light pours in like a soft rhythm.

She watches me for a moment. Just watches.
And I smile at her pendant. The delicate silver rock resting against her collarbone.
I don't mention it.
But make a quiet note to myself:
Not everything needs to be asked, Nysa. Some questions are meant to remain unanswered.

"You were beautiful in that dance last time. You and Thorne."

I freeze at his name.

"Thank you, Maisha. It was... let's say... teamwork."

A thousand thoughts, images, and sensations hit me at once.
His hand on my waist.
The heat of his marks.
His yellow eyes, glowing.
But now I see them clearly.

He is me.
The parts I feared.
The rage I swallowed.
The vulnerability I despised.
All of it. Him.

And I—I am him.
The softness. The hope. The will to dance.
Only now, more whole. More honest.

I place my hand on my belly. A wave of heat blooms from within.
My shoulders relax.

That weight...
It's gone.

Maisha watches me. And after a moment, asks—

"Still holding that picture?"

I open my hands.
The picture of a sick-looking child, curled in an old arena,

lies wrinkled between my palms.
 This—and the secret letter he left me before leaving.

Words etched in shaky ink, explaining how we need each
other:

How can one be free without the other?

A twinge in my chest—
Sadness?
Gratitude?

I lower my gaze to my arms. The marks feel quieter. And I
say nothing.

Maisha watches me gently. Then, softly:
 "Some forces are so powerful, they intuit our needs before
our eyes can see."

I lift my eyes to hers, and for once, I speak freely:
 "The truth, Maisha, is that I am not well. Yet..."
The admission settles in the air. Lighter than I expected.

She takes a breath.
 And with a smile that holds lifetimes:
 "What do you wish to do about it?"

I pause. Let the stillness settle before saying—
 "I just want to give it time."

I study her face. Her eyes. Her stillness.
And I add, with my heart bare:
"Thank you. For all you are."

She nods. And I know she understood.

"Shall we go down, Nysa?" she says, standing.
"They're about to begin the Year-End Ceremony."

As we exit the room, memories race through me—
joy, pain, collapse, endurance, clarity.

At the doorway, something catches my eye—
written in bold chalk on the blackboard:

To Nysa.
Shoutout to 202.
Where body, mind, and soul truly become whole.
~ T

My lungs fill with air. I exhale—slow, deep.
Yes. My studio, 4-202. This is home.

Downstairs, the Performance Theater glows.
White and red and gold shimmer across the room.
Professors are already seated.
The students will arrive later tonight.

In the center of the stage, I see Mr. Wolehead—
  standing on a ladder, adjusting a wall of pictures.
  Above them, a golden plaque reads Wall of Fame.

As I step closer, my heart skips.
  My photo.

My name.

And beneath it, the date:
  11.04.2025.
  Today.

"Mister Wolehead... what does this mean?"

He smiles, the proud kind. And turns to the crowd:
  "Now that she has arrived...
  Esteemed colleagues and Professors...
  I am pleased to welcome Nysa—
  as a Professor here, at The Center."

In one motion, my colleagues rise to their feet and offer a
round of applause.

"But... Mister Wolehead, everyone... what are you saying?
I was already a teacher."

He grins, eyes twinkling with delight, and tilts his head
toward Marq with a wink.
  "I believe you are now a new kind... am I told correctly?"

The clapping quiets.
 I stand still.
 My mind blanks out, suspended between wonder and disbelief.

My eyes drift upward.

"Mister Wolehead, my picture. You placed it where *his* used to be? Thorne's."

His hand rests gently on my shoulder.
 But my body doesn't flinch.
 No tension in my jaw. No weight on my shoulders.

His expression shifts—surprised.
 He noticed.
 He noticed I did not tense this time.
 And with that knowing, I smile. I wave to my colleagues.
 And in my chest: fondness. Gratitude.

He simply nods toward my portrait.
 "To your question... Was it ever about *him?*"

I turn toward him, mouth half-opened—no words come out.
 I glance over at Marq. At Maisha.
 At my picture once more.

"Oh, by the way, Nysa," he adds with a smirk,
 "I see you're not cold anymore?"

My jacket is not here. I probably left it upstairs.

"Now that I am allowed to emit a judgment," he says, voice deepening,
 "let me tell you, Nysa... I'm glad you made it. That you found your inner power. And accepted your truth.
 Our faculty would not have been the same had you not returned.
 Or worse... had you lost yourself in The Core. Let me not even imagine such a scenario."

His smile softens.
His tone shifts.

"More seriously, Nysa—watching you taught me a great lesson.
 Next time, I shall follow my intuition more. And tame it less.
 You reclaimed your place. And I owe you an apology for how I mishandled the matter with Professor Finn."

I stare at him. Silent.

He chuckles again.

"Ah, dear Nysa... if only you learnt to *see*..."
The glimmer in his eyes sharpens. Then softens.
And he lets out a long, echoing laugh.

The ceremony ends.
And the quiet settles in like a warm blanket.

Outside The Center, the wind brushes across my arms, raising goosebumps.
I rub them, squinting as the breeze stings my cheeks.

"Wait, Marq! Wait for me. I left my jacket upstairs—let me grab it quickly!"

He pauses. Looks at me.

"Oh, did you?
Maybe it just decided to return where it belonged."

I frown, puzzled.
"Decided to return...? Marq, how can a jacket decide to return..."
The words freeze on my tongue.
Don't ask, Nysa. Be open to see...

As if reading my mind, he smiles again.
I smile back.
And try another question:

"So... what will you do next year? Do you have any plans?"

"Yes, Professor. My plans remain unchanged."
He nods toward the towering building behind us.

"In some places, one can only *access* when in need.
 Some, one can only *leave* when ready."

I laugh.

"You will stay at The Center for a thirteenth year, Marq?
Are you sure?"

He smirks, already walking away.

"Oh, Professor... It is an interesting number, thirteen."

I watch him disappear into the crowd.
 A thought flickers:

One of a kind, that man.

The breeze intensifies.
I raise my face to The Sun.

That's when I see it—
 A street ad, blinking faintly in gold:

What rises when survival ends?

My pulse surges—
And then calms.

I smile. Wide.
 Without thinking, my fingers reach for the pendant at my
neck.

A warm, quiet hum pulses from it.

The golden-veined shard pendant glows faintly—
and there, slowly forming on the glass, I see:
two tiny silver thunders.

Thunders, for Thorne.

I close my eyes, gently.
 And open them wide again.

I feel whole.
 Light.
 Steady.

I take a step forward.
 And the tingling in my forearms—
 that once made me afraid, made me hide—
 returns.

But this time,
 it feels like a beginning.

A call for a new day.

THE END

A Whisper from the Author

I have learned that life is a journey where marks, scars, and cryptic whispers belong.
Were they meant to break us? Or to make us rise?

That, dear reader, is for us to define.

I leave you with a quote that found me in my darkest hours:
"To the light that has saved the world, I shall now return your shadow.
A light that embraces the shadow will never be lost in darkness."
— *Alchemy of Souls*

May you embrace light and darkness. I found them to be the foundation of our resilience.

From one wounded warrior to another.
Much love,

~Salimatou

The Path You Uncovered

I- *"What stirs when the hollow cracks?"*
1. The Cues we Cut
2. The Motion we Mute
3. The Instinct we Ignore
4. The Body we Bully
5. The Essence we Exhaust

II- *"What is seen when the veil is gone?"*
6. The Truth we Twist
7. The Core we Corrupt
8. The Bond we Bury
9. The Force we Flee
10. The Potential we Prevent
11. The Soul we Suppress

III- *"What was never meant to be carried?"*
12. The Scars we Shun
13. The Power we Permit
14. The Legacy we Loathe
15. The Stress we Silence
16. The Darkness we Deny

IV- *"What is chosen when all paths open?"*
17. The Fires we Fight
18. The Depths we Dare
19. The Feelings we Face

Personal Reflections Space

Dear Reader,
 This space is yours.
It will take you through the six pillars of resilience of our gifted model, covered in the story of Nysa and Thorne.

It is yours to reflect. To feel. To write or to rest.
 To process, or to simply *let go*.

R1

I — What stirs when the hollow cracks?

The answer is the first key pillar of our journeys of resilience: **Energy**.

Your energy is *everywhere*. It is your birthright.
 It lives in the sensations in your body, the signals you sense, the way you move, the thoughts you allow, the instincts that rise up when you need it.
 There is no *Self* without Energy.

Dear reader, like Nysa, you've likely had moments where you pushed too far. Ignored the whispers. Silenced the signals.
 We all have them. And like Nysa, you're not broken — you're becoming.

But here's what we forget: **Energy is finite.**
 Let's learn to protect it.

Your notes, doodles, or passing thoughts:

🔑 **Try**

Stand or sit. Plant your feet firmly on the ground.
Close your eyes.
Slowly scan your body from your toes to your head.
Breathe in deeply.
With every exhale, imagine sending warmth and
energy into the places that feel tense or tired.
Then pause.
Ask yourself: *What is my body telling me right now?*

🔍 **Reflect**

- When was the last time you truly trusted your
  body's instinct?

- What energy are you holding right now... that
  doesn't belong to you?

🎁 **Gift Yourself**
The gift of **movement**.

A walk. A stretch.
Or simply, a glass of water, sipped on your couch.
Give your energy *back to yourself* — if only for a
moment.

R2

II — What is seen when the veil is gone?

What makes us... is what's *within*.
It is our second pillar of resilience: **Identity**.

Your identity is indelible.
 It can be hidden behind masks, but never erased.

It lives in your beliefs.
In the pieces you show to the world — and the ones
you keep buried. In the bond you form with your true
self, the one behind the curtain.
Your Self encompasses all that is visible and invisible.

Dear reader, remember the moments when you tucked
pieces of yourself away — out of fear, or shame, or to
simply survive. We all do it.
 We cling to the traits that sparkle... and hide the ones
that ache.

But Identity can only thrive in Truth. In *wholeness*.
 Let's learn to re-embrace every part of ourselves.

Your notes, doodles, or passing thoughts:

🔑 Try

Stand tall in front of a mirror. Really look.
Into your eyes, ask: *What do I need to hear right now?*

Then, close your eyes. Breathe deeply.
And with each exhale, imagine gently shedding the layers — the doubt, the fear, the expectations.
Let yourself feel what's underneath.

🔍 Reflect

- What parts of you have been hidden — on purpose, or by habit?

- When did you first start wearing a mask? What would it take to begin taking it off now?

🎁 Gift Yourself
The gift of **truth**.

Write one affirmation that feels *honest* about who you are today.
Not perfect. Not socially acceptable. Just *true*.
Place it somewhere visible — let it remind you of your wholeness.

Your notes, doodles, or passing thoughts:

R3

III — What was never meant to be carried?
What limits us... until we limit it.
 Our third pillar for resilience: **Trauma**.

*Note: Because we never want to revisit trauma without a supportive
environment led by a trained guide, this section is designed to help you gently
brush against the surface. Think of these as the Traces left by Trauma—what
remains visible or felt, even when the event itself is long past.*

These Traces are potent.
Like The Jacket in Nysa's story—alive, insistent—they
mold us as they please.
 From the way we react to life, to the memories coded
in body and mind, to the emotional echoes that still
replay today... these traces shape how we interpret the
past, navigate the present, and anticipate the future.

Dear reader, think of those moments when you quiet
your stress, carry pain that isn't fully yours, shrink
from the light, or—like Nysa—pretend your marks
don't exist. We all feel the weight of these chains.

**Yet, as strong as they may be, they only hide your
true strength.** They begin to fade when we see what
is behind.
Let's learn to reframe the weight.
 And to reclaim what was always yours: your strength.

Your notes, doodles, or passing thoughts:

🔑 **Try**

Take a blank piece of paper.
 Consider these five elements:
 A Scar. A Dormant Power. A Heavy Chain. A Knot. A Shadow.
 Write one word—or draw one shape—for each.
 Ask yourself:
 What do I want to leave on this paper forever?

🔍 **Reflect**

- If your Dormant Power could speak, what would it say to you?

- On a scale of 1 to 10, how much energy are you spending just to carry things? What would it feel like to let even part of that go?

🎁 **Gift yourself**

The gift of **hope**.

Remember one thing you've already done—that your past self would've thought impossible.
 Now, write down one action you think you cannot do today. Keep it.
 Your future self might just thank you for achieving it.

Your notes, doodles, or passing thoughts:

R4

IV — What is chosen when all paths open?

The silent choice everything else waits for... the true turning point.
Our fourth pillar for resilience: the **Desire to be Self.**

From the moment we are born, we *are.*
Being is passive—it simply happens. But *becoming*?
That's a decision. One we make again and again.

That choice—to be yourself—is the foundation of your strength, sense of purpose, and confidence.
It lives in the quiet moments when you choose to keep going. In the silent fires you fight. In the fears you face. In the help you agree to receive. The light you let flicker—even on your darkest days.

Dear reader, remember those moments when you stood tall despite the fear? When you dared to prioritize your voice? That spark is still in you.
 It never really fades.It waits for your permission to rise again.

Without that decision, we can hardly find this light.
Let's learn to honor that decision. And make it again.
Today. Tomorrow. Every day.

Your notes, doodles, or passing thoughts:

🔑 **Try**

Stand up.

Say your full name out loud—firm, clear, and proud.

Now say:

> "I choose to be [Insert your Name]"
> "And... [Add whatever truth feels most
> alive in you right now]"

🔍 **Reflect**

- In what ways have you confused survival with living?

- When do you feel most fully alive? What tends to get in the way?

🎁 **Gift yourself**

The gift of **sovereignty**. Choose your declaration:

Turn on your favorite song, and dance like no one's watching.

Text someone you admire with something bold and empowering.

Go outside and write your name on the sidewalk, in the sand, with leaves or stones. Whatever reminds you: *I decided to exist. And I own it.*

Your notes, doodles, or passing thoughts:

R5

V — What stands when all is seen?

What follows the decision to become... is the courage to be *seen*.
 Our fifth pillar of resilience: the **Face**.

The one you show when you meet the gaze of others. Fully. Unapologetically.

Your Face—the image you show others—is sacred.
 To you. To others. To society.
 It is the gateway to the most basic human need: to be seen, recognized, accepted.

It's shaped by the stories you share, the paths you follow, the 'no' you suppress. By the space you don't take. The silence you hold. The way you twist your truth to avoid rejection.

Over time, your real 'you' learns what to shrink, erase, or mask... just to survive the scrutiny.
 Until adapting becomes *changing*.
 Until survival becomes self-erasure.

Dear reader, think of those moments when you hold your tongue to avoid mockery.
 When you edit your dreams just to fit in.
 When you doubt your worth because someone else

didn't see it.

When you rewrite your story to make it more palatable.

We've all internalized the need to adapt.

But it is only when your image stops being rewritten—that you begin writing it for yourself.
Let's learn to show up. As is.
To *face* the world without flinching, without editing, without asking for permission.

Your notes, doodles, or passing thoughts:

....

....

....

....

....

....

....

....

....

....

....

....

🔑 **Try**

Practice noticing. In your next interaction today,
quietly observe what's happening *within* you.
Do you feel your body shrink? Your voice lowered?
Are your words being filtered? Your truth edited?

Without judgment, ask yourself: *Is this really me?*
Or who I think they want to see?

🔍 **Reflect**

- When you feel judged or misunderstood, what
  story do you start telling yourself—about your
  identity? About your worth?

- What happens inside you when you say *no*?
  Choose yourself over others' expectations?

🎁 **Gift Yourself**

The gift of **authenticity**.

In your closet, choose something that feels like
you—not something you'd wear to please, prove, or
perform. Maybe it's bold. Strange. Unfashionable.
It doesn't need to make sense to anyone else.
Let it remind you: *Today, I show up for me.*

R6

VI — What rises when survival ends?

Where freedom begins.
 Where healing deepens.
 Where self-love finally takes root.
Our sixth and final pillar of resilience: the **Guide to Transformation.**

This guide is not someone else.
 It is *you.*
 It's the voice inside that was once silenced or ignored—now fully present, clear, and undeniable.

It awakens when you're no longer driven by trauma.
 When you stop surviving your past.
 When you no longer bend to the projections of others.

This guide lives in your quiet endurance.
 In your strength to forgive what fractured you.
 In your wisdom to come home to yourself.
 And in the gifts you can now see—gifts that were always within.

There is no transformation without this inner guide.
 It leads you *forward.*

Dear reader, like Nysa, **were you ever really broken?** The choices are now yours to make—once you learn to understand, appreciate, and honor your story.

Let's stop surviving. Let's begin to thrive.

Your notes, doodles, or passing thoughts:

....

....

....

....

....

....

....

....

....

....

....

....

....

....

....

....

....

....

🔑 Try

Find a beautiful piece of paper.
Write a letter to yourself—a younger version of you.

It could be you from 20 years ago, 5 years ago, or just months ago... when your journey toward transformation began.

Start the letter with:

"Dear [Your First Name]"

Write it in first person. Speak from the heart.
Thank them. Tell them what you know now.
Share what you hope for the future.
Say what they never got to hear.

When you're done, fold it.
Keep it safe.

🔍 Reflect

- What are you quietly outgrowing?

- What do you now know about yourself that no one—not even life—can take from you?

🎁 Gift Yourself

The gift of **becoming**.

Choose a small object that symbolizes your growth—
Like Nysa's shard. Like Maisha's pendant.
A stone. A bracelet. A ring. A note.

Something meaningful.
Something that says: *I've journeyed. I've changed. I am becoming.*

Keep it close. Let it remind you:

You are the guide you were waiting for.

Your notes, doodles, or passing thoughts:

....

....

....

....

....

....

....

....

....

....

....

About the Author

Salimatou Baldé

Salimatou Baldé is a certified coach in confidence and resilience, an international speaker, educator, and founder of *gifted*—a transformative space created to help adults navigate identity, purpose, and self-worth.

With over a decade of experience in Learning & Development, she has guided thousands of individuals through personal and professional transformation within the United Nations, public institutions, and private organizations.

Salimatou's own journey with Sickle Cell Disease (SCD), combined with her work as a coach and 14 years of volunteer service with NGOs, shaped her deep understanding of what it means to endure, adapt, and rise. These experiences inspired the creation of the **gifted model**: six pillars of resilience designed to help others turn scars into strength.

Outside her professional work, Salimatou finds joy in salsa dancing—Porto and Cuban styles—having danced for over 11 years. She is also a passionate reader of mystery and romance novels, and enjoys traveling between her current home in Spain and her roots in France.